Looking for Homer

Finding the Trojan War

Manuel Robbins

LOOKING FOR HOMER
FINDING THE TROJAN WAR

Copyright © 2017 Manuel Robbins.

All rights reserved. No part of this book may be used or reproduced by any means, graphic, electronic, or mechanical, including photocopying, recording, taping or by any information storage retrieval system without the written permission of the author except in the case of brief quotations embodied in critical articles and reviews.

iUniverse books may be ordered through booksellers or by contacting:

iUniverse
1663 Liberty Drive
Bloomington, IN 47403
www.iuniverse.com
1-800-Authors (1-800-288-4677)

Because of the dynamic nature of the Internet, any web addresses or links contained in this book may have changed since publication and may no longer be valid. The views expressed in this work are solely those of the author and do not necessarily reflect the views of the publisher, and the publisher hereby disclaims any responsibility for them.

Any people depicted in stock imagery provided by Thinkstock are models, and such images are being used for illustrative purposes only. Certain stock imagery © Thinkstock.

ISBN: 978-1-5320-2048-3 (sc)
ISBN: 978-1-5320-2049-0 (e)

Library of Congress Control Number: 2017904679

Print information available on the last page.

iUniverse rev. date: 05/30/2017

*To my grandsons
Eric and Zachary*

*There are mysteries
That have come to us from
The deep past*

CONTENTS

Preface vii

    1. Introduction 1
    2. The Poet-Singer 16
    3. When Homer Lived 28
    4. Time of the Trojan War 42
    5. From the Hittite Records 50
    6. Opportunity and Adventure 68
    7. The War at Troy 75
    8. Orality and Tradition 87
    9. Venue 97
  10. Writing and Transmission 108

Afterword 115

Notes 117

Appendices 131

Readings 151

Index 161

PREFACE

Iliad and *Odyssey* are the oldest surviving works of European literature and therefore of Western literature. The Greeks of the Classical period considered these to be their greatest works. So Aristotle testified, making a judgment based on aesthetics. So the ages have ratified, since these works survive to our time, while nearly all others have faded away except for surviving text fragments. Whether both of these were composed by Homer, is guesswork. The ancients thought so, but they supposed many other works to be by him. A modern bookshelf has translations into English of *Iliad* and *Odyssey* and both works are labeled as by Homer. Yet today there is less certainty that one man—Homer—composed both. I have doubts that *Odyssey* is by Homer. Or is it the other way around? The issue is unsolvable and I put it aside as unproductive. In this small book, only *Iliad* will be considered.

The literary merit of Iliad is not covered in this book. Much has been written about that. It is summarized in a work by Smith and Miller (see Readings).

> The Iliad is not a short poem. The wrath with its various episodes and the warring of heroes, requires 15,693 hexameter verses. But it is not the bulk of the Iliad that makes it immortal but the majesty and beauty of the poetry, the melody of the meter, the simplicity of the language, the dramatic power of its structure, and the profoundness of the thought. Homer knew how to sound the heights and depths of every human

experience, and his poem abounds in passages of exquisite beauty, vivid description, touching pathos, eloquent speeches, the words and deeds of knightly heroes whose whole ambition was ever to be the best.

Iliad is a war story. It is unsurpassed in literature in the sense of immediacy that it provides. The action is happening here and now. The tale is told, or sung for this is a poetic work, in such specific and vivid detail that one can hardly help but thinking that this is a report of an actual war—a report from the battle front.

Iliad is, in certain ways, not a perfect work. There are such mechanical problems as a story rupture during the "embassy" to Achilles, or the Catalog of Ships inserted oddly into the text, and there are frequent minor self-contradictions. The plot is strange, dealing as it does with a great warrior—Achilles—who does virtually nothing through much of the story. The story is full of pathos. The ancient audience knew that the Greek Achilles was doomed from the beginning. Humans seek to control their destinies, but the gods dispose. Gods believe that they control, but they do not, for over them is Fate. Agamemnon, chief of the Greek forces, is doomed though that is not worked out within *Iliad*. Not only is Trojan Hector doomed, but so are his whole family—father, brothers, wife, children—and all the other Trojans. That also is not worked out in *Iliad*, but it is clear enough from other works related *to Iliad*.

Iliad deals with the carnage of battle in painful detail. The slaughter is amply described and is gruesome, but the constant repetition seems aimed at making the listener sick of war. From this it is possible to believe that Homer was a pacifist. Homer has great, almost overwhelming, sympathy for Priam and his family and the

Trojans. Their side of the story is told without rancor, and not in a way that one ordinarily tells of an enemy.

This, then, is the work so appreciated by the ancients, and moderns. Its composition is fraught with mysteries. We love mysteries because they challenge us. We hate mysteries because we cannot solve them. They hide something from us, and that is something we cannot stand. They tax our limited knowledge and mental powers.

That is why this investigation was undertaken. There are so many problems. How could such a great work appear seemingly out of nothing? There are no antecedents that we know of. Where did the war story come from? Was there a Trojan War? Who was Homer? Where did he come from and when did he live? Why did the ancients know so little about him? Did he live in the Greek Dark Age, an age without writing? If so, how do we have a written *Iliad*? How did it come down to us from ancient times? These are some of the mysteries.

In a way it seems futile to delve into these matters, or into anything dealing with Homer or *Iliad*. Even in ancient times, Homer was written about frequently. In modern times, with so many able scholars at work in Homeric studies, the mass of books and scholarly papers produced is so huge that if they were piled up, one on top of the other, they would challenge the heights of Mount Olympus. There is hardly a declarative sentence in this book that could not bring forth from the accumulated scholarship one or more references, one or more footnotes. I offer this work only because it may provide some slightly different insights. I do not believe that I have solved all of the problems mentioned above. But the search for answers has helped me to understand Homer's work better, and some of the mystery has given way to a reasonable clarity.

1

INTRODUCTION

What will be discussed happened far away and long ago and it may be useful to explain place and time. Two locations are of interest. There is, of course, Greece. Ancient Greece was not a country in the modern sense. There was hardly ever a Greek nation in ancient times, a unified land under a single rule, but rather a number of city-states separately ruled. Ancient Greece is best understood as the place or places where Greeks lived in large numbers. Who were the Greeks? They were those who spoke the Greek language, shared certain religious beliefs and shrines, and saw one another as kindred. That region so defined would include what today is the Greek mainland, and also in certain periods Greek populations in Crete, Cyprus, and southern Italy. There were also Greeks across the Aegean Sea, on the west coast of Anatolia, and that is most important.

Anatolia is the name by which Turkey is known in ancient times, before the arrival of the Turks in the region. In the earliest time period of interest here, the dominant people of Anatolia were the Hittites, people of Hittite speech, the earliest known and recorded member of the Indo-European family of languages. Around them in Anatolia lived peoples who spoke kindred languages, Palaic to the north, and Luvian to the west along the Aegean coast. Troy, the city whose fame is entirely due to Homer, was located on the west coast of Anatolia.

Several time periods are discussed here. As an aid to understanding what will be said, following, these are briefly described.

The Greek Bronze Age

Homer seemingly knew of what is now called the Bronze Age, and refers to it though he lived centuries after that period. It may seem strange that an important period in the past is named after a metal alloy—bronze—yet this metal alloy did play more than a merely practical role in daily life. Bronze was used in arms and armor, pots and pans, and many and various hardware needs. Iron was barely known at that time. The technology of extracting iron from its ores was a difficult one. The Hittites had mastered it, and apparently no one else. It was a rare metal, and a Hittite king sent an iron dagger as a prized gift to another king. To make bronze, copper and tin were needed. The search for these metals over land and sea, over centuries of the Bronze Age, led to adventurous exploration and international trade, defining factors of the Bronze Age.

The Late Bronze Age is dated here to 1600 BC to 1200 BC.[11] In Egypt, great temples were built during this period, but not the pyramids, which were already ancient by this time. Illustrations and writing in hieroglyphics on Egyptian temple walls provide a good outline of Late Bronze Egyptian history.

To the north of Egypt along the coast, small city states existed corresponding to what today is Israel, Lebanon, and Syria. These were all literate states, even as early as the Bronze Age, meaning that professional scribes were available who could serve the writing needs of people of all classes, who were otherwise illiterate. Those peoples, who spoke some variant of the Northwest Semitic language, left little of grand or monumental structures behind during the Bronze Age for the archaeologist to discover.

There were small cities, small palaces, but there was not in that region in that period a sufficient economic basis to encourage a great conqueror who might demand grandiose sculptures, or vast temples.

North of Canaan, Anatolia of the Late Bronze Age is all important for matters discussed in this book. Hittites were the dominant force in Anatolia, ruling from Hattusa, their capital in central Anatolia, the remains of which can still be seen east of present-day Ankara. These ruins suggest that Hattusa was an all but impregnable fortress city. The location of Hattusa on a high prairie, near a river running in a deep gorge from which canals could not draw water, meant that the Hittites had a weak agricultural base and a weak economy. This is not the situation from which ordinarily a great power emerges, yet the Hittites were a great power of the Late Bronze Age. In the 1300s BC, in the time of Egyptian king Ramesses II, the Hittites and the Egyptians were the two super powers of that time. Hittite strength was based on skillfully arranged treaties with virtually all nearby states, by economic and mutual defense treaties with these states, and by the threat of Hittite armies when other measures failed.

Map A. Certain cities of the Greek Bronze Age, most of them fortified.

Looking for Homer

Hittite interests were primarily directed to the southeast, to the several small kingdoms in Syria. These states furnished the Hittites with tribute, all important to Hittite economic survival. To the west, by contrast, in the direction of the Aegean Sea, and Troy, Hittite interest was more to ensuring stability, to "protect their back." It was under the circumstance of frequent unrest in the west that the Hittites first encountered the Greeks.

Hittite central rule in Anatolia came to a mysterious end shortly after 1200 BC. The Hittites were no more heard of in history after that time, though they left a descendent state in southern Anatolia known as Turhuntassa, and another, Kargamish, in Syria.[1,2] (See also the author's *Collapse of the Bronze Age* for further information. Listed in Readings)

In Greece, the most obvious aspect of Bronze Age civilization is the great palaces. The most impressive of these is at Mycenae (Map A). Here, the palace was within the walls of a great fortress on a high hill. The ruins at this site are imposing and impressive even today. Not far away to the south at Tiryns was another fortress, almost as imposing as that at Mycenae. On the west coast of the Greek mainland at Pylos are the remains of a palace often referred to as the Palace of Nestor after a major character in *Iliad*. That it is called the Palace of Nestor is an example of the influence of Homer on archaeological-historical thinking, and by no means the only example. No matter. Little harm is done, except when the works of Homer are taken too literally as history.

The palace at Pylos contained a central hall, a large circular hearth and probably a chimney suspended above, and richly colored frescos painted on the walls. A storeroom contained a large number of kylixes, stemmed drinking cups, and these might have been manufactured locally and held for trade. There was an archive room in which were stored economic records, recorded on clay, baked hard in a later fire that consumed Pylos. These records, written in Linear B, to be further discussed later, indicate that there existed a tightly controlled economic system in which raw materials and expected finished products were assigned to workers in a quota system. Certain Pylos Linear B tablets deal with seemingly special preparations for coastal defense. In the end, defensive measures did not avail. The palace was destroyed in the upheaval of the end of the Greek Bronze Age.

Mycenae has given its name to the Age, the Mycenaean Age, roughly equivalent to the Greek Late Bronze Age. Mycenae was, of course, the seat of Agamemnon, King of Men, according to Homer. At Mycenae, the situation appears to have been very similar to that at Pylos. There was within the circuit of the great walls a group of graves, and higher up a palace, and perhaps more than one palace, hearths, frescos. In buildings just outside the walls there was oil storage and Linear B tablets. The existence of tablets suggests, as at Pylos, a centrally managed economy. The strong walls indicate a concern for defense. In the end, it did not avail. Nor did the strong walls of Tiryns. At Mycenae and Tiryns the palaces were destroyed.

Sparta, according to Homer, was the location of the palace of Menelaus, brother of Agamemnon. A Bronze Age tomb has been discovered in the vicinity in which was found marvelous drinking cups fashioned of gold. The remains of a Bronze Age palace has been found containing frescos, tablets with Linear B writing, objects of gold, and bronze swords.

There was also a palace on the acropolis of Athens, and probably at Thebes, Iolkos, Gla. Overseas, after about 1450 BC, the place at Knossos in Crete can be counted among the Greek palaces. Also overseas, there was a palace at Troy. So far as one can judge from the works of Homer, the Trojans spoke perfectly good Greek. That, however, must be considered a storyteller's necessity, since the story told in *Iliad* would not have been possible without easy communications between Greek and Trojan. It is unlikely that the Trojans were Greek. Far more likely is that the Trojans were typical Anatolians and spoke a Luvian dialect, like their neighbors in western Anatolia.

Source of Wealth in the Palaces

Construction and upkeep of fortresses and palaces obviously required a source of wealth. Judging from the Linear B records, a great number of people were employed in numerous trades, managed from the palaces. Wine, pottery, textiles are among the products, and there was likely much more. A relatively large population, some living close to the palace, many living on the outlying land, is implied. Trade was probably the main source of wealth, and Greek pottery of the Bronze Age has been found as far away as Egypt. Hittite records indicate that Greek ships were reaching Syria and offloading cargo there. The Hittite king put a stop to that. But wealth may have come from more than trade. The Greek kingdoms, or kingdom if they were at that time under the rule of one king, seem to have been expansionist, seizing opportunities where opportunities presented themselves. That would explain the sudden emergence of Greek rule in Crete. It would explain an aggressive behavior of Greeks along the west coast of Anatolia. Here, along the coast, they would have become aware of Hittites, and of Troy.

The Strange Circumstance of Writing

The story of how Michael Ventris decrypted the previously mysterious Linear B texts is well known (see Chadwick 1958 in

Readings). Over three thousand Linear B tablets have been found at Knossos in Crete, and more than a thousand from Pylos, and lesser numbers at Mycenae and Thebes. This is taken to be the writing system of Greece in the Bronze Age. But can that be so? All experts who have examined the matter would agree that Linear B was very poorly suited to record the Greek tongue. In other lands of the Late Bronze Age, subjects of writing included diplomatic correspondence and treaties, deeds, business transactions, legal findings, medical formulas, prayers, magic spells, personal letters, poetry, epic story. None of these have ever been found in Linear B tablets. Only dry accounting records are known.

Greek kings exchanged correspondence with Hittite kings, as will be discussed in Chapter 5. How was this done? What writing system was used? It could not have been Linear B. Was it accomplished in an Anatolian writing system such as Luvian hieroglyphs or Hittite cuneiform? It is difficult to believe that with diplomatic relations between Greek and Hittite, with practicality and prestige involved, that the Greeks of the Late Bronze Age had no efficient writing system of their own with which to communicate. It must be assumed that there was such a Greek writing system though evidence of it has never been found. Greeks did not write on temple walls and, indeed, there were no temples. One must assume that there was writing on a perishable material, but Greece is not a land in which perishable materials would have survived from the Bronze Age.

It may be wondered, why didn't the Greek accountants use this supposed Greek writing system, if it existed. The answer may be that Linear B had the advantage of being compact since it did not represent all speech sounds. Thus, Linear B was handy for short lists written on small clay tablets. Further, the use of Linear B gave the accountants a professional jargon of their own, just as a few generations ago doctors used Latin to write prescriptions.

Because true Greek writing of the Late Bronze Age has never been found, and possibly never existed, Greek history of that time is completely unknown. The names of kings in Egypt, Anatolia, Canaan, Assyria are known. But the name of not one king of Bronze Age Greece is known from any contemporary record. Much that passes for Greek history of the Bronze Age is dependent on Homer—for that purpose a very frail reed indeed—or on mythological tales, or on archaeological findings which are, in the absence of writing, simply not up to that task.

It is not to Greece, therefore, that one must turn in order to validate what Homer says of the Bronze Age or of a Trojan War.

The Dark Age of Greece

The palace based society of Late Bronze Age Greece came to a mysterious end somewhat after 1200 BC. For some time scholars thought the collapse of the Mycenaean world was due to "invaders." There is little or no evidence to support that view. More than before, scholars are beginning to accept that an enduring adverse turn of the climate will destroy—and has destroyed—civilizations, by destroying the agricultural basis of existence, or by unleashing devastating epidemic, and by injuring social order. That fate best fits the known situation of the Mycenaean world. At about the same time, there were serious problems in Anatolia, Cyprus, Canaan, and Egypt.

The result was a terrible regressive period in Greece. Linear B records were no longer kept and this seems to signal the end of the palace-centered management of the economy which had functioned for centuries. If the palace ceased to manage the economy, it is safe to say that the palace no longer ruled.

After widespread abandonment and destruction, society struggled to right itself. In the greatly damaged citadel of Mycenae, a feeble attempt at reconstruction took place, and with it a revival in skilled pottery work. Then, following some further damage, the resurgence lost its drive. In Tiryns, the citadel was all but abandoned after 1190 BC, and life only resumed to a degree in an expanded lower town. Greece sank irreversibly into a profound depression that lasted for centuries. This introduced the Greek Dark Age, dark because of economic circumstances, and dark because so little is known about that period.

The land was so impoverished, so lacking in material possessions, that archaeologists have found little which would illuminate those times. Great buildings were not built, and houses were of the simplest sort, hardly more than huts. Frescos were not painted, gemstones or ivory were not carved, bronze became scarce and was replaced in part by iron. Pottery design and execution degenerated, though in Athens, which was perhaps less affected by the collapse, new designs were pioneered. There was no writing, even in the alphabetic script which came into Greece later.

An infrequent trade still existed in this period. Objects from oversees, evidence of trade, are scarce in the archaeological record, though Athenian pottery of the period has been found in Cyprus. Somewhat later, there was a short but lucrative trade between Euboea on east of the Greek mainland and the Syrian coast, but it did not relieve the general gloom in the rest of Greece. Other than some pottery, it is difficult to see what Greece might have had in those times that others might want. Population numbers collapsed. The number of settlements in mainland Greece of that period which archaeologists have found number little more than a few dozen, in contrast to the five hundred known settlements at the end of the Bronze Age. All aspects of high culture were gone. It is a question whether what remained can still be considered civilization, so severe seems the regression.

However terrible the times, and severe the depopulation of mainland Greece, certain core elements of Bronze Age Greek culture were preserved. These were language; the names of many of the gods; memories of the Bronze Age; mythology; poet-singers' work which would later form the basis of Homer's work; and likely much more which cannot now be identified.

By that time, a new configuration of population existed in the Greek world. The collapse was followed by emigrations, beginning perhaps around 1100 BC. Greeks had sailed for new shores, including the shores of Anatolia where perhaps better land existed. Depending on the part of mainland Greece from which they came, these Greeks brought different dialects with them. To the north along the west coast of Anatolia, including the island of Lesbos, the dialect was Aeolic. Further south along the coast the dialect was Ionic. Ionic, closely related to the Athenian or Attic dialect, was also spoken in Euboea (see Map B).

Map B. Two important Greek dialects located on both sides of the Aegean Sea and established before the Classical period.

Recovery Period

No special time span can be allocated to this regressive period, but signs of some recovery were evident by about 800 BC. As Greece began to emerge from this decline, Athens and the Ionian-speaking cities of Anatolia seem to have led the way. Homer lived at some time after the beginning of recovery, and the Phoenician alphabet began to be adopted among Greek-speaking people.

Objects found in graves show that trade with the Syrian coast had picked up, and near 750 BC a Greek trading post was established at Al Mina at the mouth of the Orontes River. In following years, Greeks appear as mercenaries in the East and in the navy of Pharaoh Necho in Egypt, which indicates that once again population growth and population pressure were developing in Greece. Cultural developments become clearer. Notable lyric poets flourished, and their works were in writing. The writing system came from Phoenicia. There was a stir in the Greek world, at last, culminating in the astonishing Classical period.

Classical Period

By 500 BC, Persia ruled most of the civilized world. Greek cities in Anatolia came under the rule of the Persians. Athens, expressing a kinship with the Ionian Greek cities of western Anatolia, encouraged a revolt. The revolt failed. Irritated by Athenian meddling, the Persians attempted a punitive raid against Athens. Landing at Marathon across a narrow peninsula from Athens, the Persian force was defeated on the beach by the Athenians. The Persians then organized a massive invasion of Greece. In 480 BC, they reached Thermopylae where they were delayed by the resolute Spartans. They reached Athens shortly after, and burned the city. However, in a battle at sea just beyond Athenian shores, the Persian fleet was defeated and much of the Persian force withdrew. In a decisive land battle the next year, Persia was defeated. This spelled the end of the direct Persian threat to mainland Greece.

The victory over this great superpower led to a burst of self-confidence and optimism in Athens which played a catalytic role in the blossoming of the Classical period, the most accomplished period of Greek civilization. It was in this period that the great play-wrights, historians, sculptors, and many of the philosophers lived and worked.

From this time, the story of Greece is fully historical, and no more need be said here about time periods.

Early Origin of Hero Tales

Stories, poems, songs of valiant men are older than Greece, older than civilization, ages old. In France, at Lascaux, there are caves in which have been found marvelous drawings of animals. The art is of great skill, and though features of the animals are in some cases exaggerated, it is obvious that this was the artist's intent, and that he had full control of his art. A few pictures show humans. One such picture shows men with bow and arrows facing deer. Another shows a large bull with a man prostrate before him. The man is obviously dead. These are stories told in pictures. Who can doubt that these pictures illustrate a story also told verbally, and that men told of valorous deeds far back in time. It is estimated that these cave pictures were painted in the Paleolithic, about twenty thousand years ago.

It is not necessary or possible to trace the history of telling of heroic deeds from the Paleolithic to earliest Greece. It is sufficient to say that stories told verbally—there was no writing—were in many cases indispensable to human social existence. They played a role in society beyond entertainment, as they explained and affirmed social values and norms, and reinforce existing beliefs. In the Bronze Age palace at Pylos, there was a fresco of an individual playing a lyre and before her—the figure may be a Muse—at the level of her head, a bird is shown flying away as if from her face. The bird, winging away, in all probability is a visual representation of Story or Song. This may illustrate the "winged words," an enigmatic expression often found in Homer's work. This fresco was located in what is believed to be the Throne Room, the place were men would gather, where they would be entertained. Stories of valor would be expected, just as is told in *Odyssey* as King Alcinous calls for Demodocus who sings of the heroes of Troy.

This fresco illustrates that Greeks of the Mycenaean period were telling tales of combat and valor hundreds of years before Homer. Somehow, stories from the Bronze Age were preserved through the Dark Age, perhaps distorted by the passage of time, and were known to Homer. Homer knew stories from many sources and times. He was a master of narrative, using creative methods formed over generations.

2

THE POET-SINGER

His works have been in writing for centuries, and when the text is read aloud, at least the text in Greek, it is clear that it is poetry. Thus, generations have called Homer a poet. However, as modern scholarship has made clear, the works were originally meant for performance before an audience. For that reason, in recent years, the term "singer" has been applied. Thus the term "poet-singer" is an apt description and is the term used here. "Bard" has a similar meaning but is best reserved for Celtic or English performers of a different kind.

Though Homer and his contemporary performers are called poet-singers, they did not "sing" as we usually understand the term. It isn't certain how they delivered their words, but it is likely that it was a near monotone or chant of a few fixed notes suitable to the verse, accompanied by a strum of the lyre. The lyre provided emphasis as the performer needed and, by inducing a pause when needed, allowed the performer a moment to think and to catch his breath. As for the term "poet," Homer's was no ordinary poetry. It was not in rhyme. And unlike most poetry in English, Homeric verse was in dactylic hexameter, and that is its most important characteristic.

The verse was clothed in a traditional poetic language or diction, adapted for the purpose over years, perhaps centuries, containing evidence of several Greek dialects, containing also some word modifications, syllable stretches, all this in order to meet the difficult demands of the meter. It was a conservative language reflecting generations of use.

The poet-singer learned his craft by listening to an established poet-singer, and adopting his methods and poetic language. The poetic language was slowly updated over the years, approximating the dialect of ordinary speech, but updated only where the new would meet the meter as well as did the older words replaced. To Homer's listeners, the language would have had a quaint and slightly archaic sound, as Victorian poetry does to our ears. To Athenians centuries later, when the works of Homer were recited, they would have had a decidedly archaic sound, an elevated or monumental tone, probably as the King James Bible sounds to us.

Orality

While the works of Homer have been subject to scholarly scrutiny since ancient times, the most remarkable results achieved by scholarship have been within recent decades. This scholarship provides insight into how the Homeric poet-singer employed his craft. Certain poetic lines, certain word groups, certain vocabulary have been counted and subject to statistical analysis resulting in remarkable findings. Because this work is quantitative, it places some aspects of Homeric scholarship nearly at the level of a science. The names Milman Parry, Alfred Lord, and Richard Janko are among those who are prominent in this work.

Parry observed that certain poetic verse lines were repeated through *Iliad* and *Odyssey*, about a third of all lines. There are many examples. Thus, to introduce a new day-

> *Now when the earth-born rose-fingered Dawn has arisen.*

is used frequently in *Iliad*. For a death in combat-

> *Down he fell with a crash, and his armor clattered about him.*

And if some verses are not exactly identical, then they are nearly so through the change of a word or two.

Within other verse lines there were also repeats. A poetic line might, for example, be about the Trojan champion Hector. Alternatively, "Hector of the shining helm" or "glorious Hector" could be used, depending on which fulfilled the meter of the verse line. And these expressions might be used again and again. Study of *Iliad* and *Odyssey* showed these to be stock phrases, employed as needed, sometimes not even making particular sense where used. These two endings, and others like them, were used throughout the works of Homer.

It is unlikely that someone long accustomed to writing would repeat whole lines of verse, would repeat stock phrases. However, the Homeric poet-singer needed these repeated lines or phrases. The reason is that, traditionally, the works were not composed in writing. They were composed by the performer, live, before an audience, and having stock lines and phrases at the ready, in his mind, made that possible.

Homer and his contemporary poet-singers could compose during performance using skills for which they had trained since childhood. First, and most important, the poet-singer was a storyteller. He could develop a story in his mind: plots, scenes, incidents, characters. Now, in his mind, verses formed, in meter. Often, he needed a stock verse line or phrase ready-made, such as those just mentioned, which he could sing with little conscious attention, and that would allow him mental space in which he could recall the plot and form the next verses. The audience was not troubled by recurring phrases or lines. It was common in this tradition of storytelling. They did not think back about a repeat or reoccurrence. The poet-singer's charisma held them in the present, in the moment.

Though he held the audience in the present, as he performed the poet-singer retained a memory of previous verses. He knew where he was in the story, and needed to be aware of where the story was going. All these demands meant that a performance of any great length would be physically taxing.

That poet-singers of Homer's time did not have, did not use, did not need a written text may seem a remarkable thing. Nor should this be a surprise. Homer appears to testify to this. In *Odyssey*, he describes a poet-singer, Demodocus, who is called to the palace to perform. He is blind and could not read. The term "orality" captures this method of story creation without writing, and to these skills.

Poet-Singers of Bosnia

But how could the orality of Homer be confirmed? Homer was not available for interview, and millennia of literacy had submerged the poet-singer's craft through most of the world. Parry heard that in Bosnia, in the Balkans, there were still poet-singers. Particularly in the rural Moslem villages, the craft was still alive. These poet-singers sang in the Serbian language.

In the early 1930's, Parry went to Bosnia. He had a plan. He knew what he must learn of their oral craft. He learned Serbian. He brought a recorder. This was an analog disc recorder using aluminum discs. The machine was powered by batteries or by a generator, state of the art equipment at that time. In general, what he learned confirmed the workings of the oral method. With selected singers, Parry could suggest a subject, and the poet singer could improvise a poem of hundreds of verses. Or, the poet singer could perform a traditional story. Or he could listen to another singer, then deliver the same story with his own color and embellishments, all without the use of writing. He need not be original. A story already known to listeners but told in a new way would be appreciated.

Parry worked with several poet-singers in Bosnia. One, Avdo Mededovic,' performed a tale which was 12,000 verse lines in length, comparable to the length of *Odyssey*. We who might, under the pressure of school, recite in the classroom from memory a poem of a few dozen lines, should find this remarkable. Avdo's performance gives credibility to the possibility that Homer could have composed *Iliad* or *Odyssey* orally, before an audience.

Another Bosnian poet-singer, Demail Zogić performed a short romantic story about a bird named Ali Bey. This was in the year 1931. He was asked to repeat the story in 1951. Both performances were recorded. The content of the two performances were substantially identical, but a few differences crept into the words used, but not in the story. To a poet-singer, this meant that the two performances were identical. The poet-singer does not know writing, and does not even understand the concept of word for word identical. To him, it is the story and its elements that are identical.

This performance by Zogić suggests continuity of memory such as might allow a story to be passed from one generation of poet-singers

Looking for Homer

to the next. It also shows that it is very unlikely that the passage from one generation to the next would be word for word.

All that Parry learned, and all that his colleague and successor, Alfred Lord learned, has confirmed orality and the remarkable capabilities of the skilled poet-singer.

Figure 1. Filip Visnjic, a Bosnian performer of the mid 1800s. In his hand is the *gusle*, the single string instrument favored by the poet-singers. He has been called the Homer of Bosnia.

The Poet-Singer at Work

Homer and the poet-singers of his time worked in hexameter. Some sense of the sound of hexameter is given in this short section below, from *Iliad* Book II, in which the Greeks are preparing for battle.[2.1]

> *Well let him sharpen his spear; well fasten the orb of his buckler;*
>
> *Well let him heap up fodder to strengthen his thundering war-steeds:*
>
> *Well let him scan his car, and himself make ready for battle:*
>
> *So that, from morn till eve, we may strive in the strife of the valiant:*
>
> *Strive with no pause between, no weak cessation or breathing:*
>
> *Strive, till the sacred night put an end to the noble contention!*

This meter provides a driving forward movement very suitable for an epic. This meter is the framework within which all of the work of the Homeric poet-singer must fit.

The poet-singer responds to the interests of the audience. He may lengthen, shorten, or change the story as he progresses. While the oral singer could, upon a challenge, compose to any theme given him on the spot, there is no requirement that he do so. More often he will know the subject upon which he will perform. Thought and planning would probably be given to the work ahead, particularly if it was to be performed on an important topic before an important audience. It is likely that, in the period before performance, a number of elements of the work would be considered by the performer, and that a good deal of the final composition worked out in his mind, before-hand. Thus, it is likely, perhaps certain, that ahead of time he developed the overall plot and decided on the main events and incidents that would give structure and weight to the work. He probably considered the character of the main personalities and how these personalities might be described, and how reflected in action. Inevitably, useful poetic lines would occur to him during these deliberations, and the more suitable ones retained in memory.

He would call to mind segments of poetry which he had received from the past from other poet-singers which might be useful, and would place these in the forefront of memory. Likewise with whole segments of his own earlier work. Many similes, with their intricate word images also may have been thought about before-hand, and these similes retained in memory. But these were not yet a story, because they lacked connection and continuity. The story would only come together during performance.

As he started the performance with the invocation, he recalled all of the above, in the order in which they would be needed. He drew upon the ability, developed over a lifetime, of forming connected thoughts and framing them in metric formulas needed to express them. He proceeded to tell the story, using lines which may not have existed until this moment of need. The poet-singers method was not pure, not purely drawn from memory, not purely composition for the first time at performance, and the idea of a pure method would have seemed to him not pragmatic and without purpose or merit.

The poet-singer may be called upon to perform a certain story again and again. It is likely that Homer was called upon to repeat certain segments of what would become *Iliad* again and again, place to place, which would have enhanced the fame of Homer and the work. There was with little doubt variation in performance to performance. *Iliad* had no rigid form. A minor character might be killed in combat in one performance and be alive in another. An activity of the gods, if not directly tied to an essential plot situation on earth, might appear in a different place, performance to performance. No two performances of *Iliad*, for example, if there ever were such, would be exactly the same.

Physical Demands

As he begins his story before an audience, the poet-singer is in his moment of strength. The work is hard. As he performs, he must be fully aware of the names of characters and places of which he tells. *Odyssey* mentions over 500 such names. He must constantly know where he has been in the story, where he is, where he is going. *Iliad* and *Odyssey* have errors in this, but very few in view of the length of these works. This demonstrates an amazing situational awareness on the part of Homer.

Based on their observations in Bosnia, Parry and Lord recognized how hard such work can be. Lord noted that, by its nature, oral performance requires rapid delivery, rapid composition. Parry notes that "It takes the full strength of a man to sing this way." He notices that the typical singer might go 20 to 40 minutes but then he would need a break. One should recall Demodocus, the singer in *Odyssey*. A goblet of wine and a basket of food were set by him for refreshment during breaks.

Looking for Homer

A Channel to the Past.

Stories came to Homer from the past, perhaps the deep past, from poet-singers over the generations. This channel appears to have reached back to the Age of Heroes, the Bronze Age in our terms, and possibly even further back. But it was a highly imperfect channel for the transmission of history. As each new generation picked up a story, certain things were easily forgotten if they were not important to that poet-singer or the audience of that day. Inevitably, current things entered the story: perhaps descriptions of clothing, the palace, and much else. As a result, and with particular reference to the tale of the Trojan War, the stories of Homer contain much that is not of the Bronze Age but of later times. Still, there is a Bronze Age content, particularly in *Iliad*. More of that in Chapter 8.

Effect of Writing

As noted earlier, the poet-singer listens to stories from the past, from earlier poet-singers over the generations. He hears, remembers, selects, and composes according to his own needs. He does not need a written text, and that is so for a remote Homer as for a recent poet-singer in Bosnia.

Yet it seems likely that Homer lived at a time when writing was in the early stages of development in Greece. It is even possible that a poet-singer of extra ordinary skills such as Homer could write, could put his own work into writing. In doing so, he would not have the stimulation and encouragement that comes from composition in performance before an audience but many of the features of pure orality would be preserved. He would think like an oral poet even as he wrote. He would form in his mind plot, characters, scenes and situations to a large extent ahead of time, just as in purely oral composition. He would use the traditional language and metrical poetic diction, all of the aids to composition that the purely oral poet-singer used, because he knew no other approach. Then, verse by verse, he would put the words into writing. A work composed this way would hardly be distinguishable from a work composed entirely orally, before an audience. A poet-singer working in this way can be thought of as a "transitional" oral performer, and Homer may have been such. This should be kept in mind, in view of what will be said in Chapter 9.

The oral poet-singer has no training as a historian, no historic resources to consult, no concept of "history" as we understand the term. He wishes to give a true report, but looks to the Muse to guide his words. The introduction of writing does not necessarily change this. In a much later age, other epics, such as Beowolf or the Song of Roland, show signs of an oral origin though reworked by literate hands. Yet they remain substantially nonhistorical and preserve the distortions and exaggerations typical of strictly oral works.

Where Homer Lived and Worked

According to the Greeks, Homer was their greatest poet, great beyond measure, yet nothing is really known about him. Some few things are learned of him indirectly. It might be better to say that only one thing is learned of him, and that is the locality in which he lived, and worked.

Simonides of Kea who lived around 470 BC wrote "The man from Chios called Homer said a beautiful thing. 'The generations of men are like leaves of a tree.'" This seems to reflect verses from *Iliad*:

> *As is the generation of leaves, so is that of humanity*
>
> *The wind scatters the leaves on the ground, but the live timber*
>
> *Burgeons with leaves again in the season of spring returning.*

Here, Simonides places Homer on Chios. Chios is an island just off the western coast of Anatolia, and was culturally part of Ionia (Map B). This view is strongly supported by the Greek dialect that Homer used, the dialect in which *Iliad* and *Odyssey* are composed. That dialect is Ionic. Simonides' statement supports the claim of Anatolian Ionia as the land of Homer, as against Athens and others that also claimed him.[22] This makes it nearly certain, as certain as such prehistorical matters can be. Homer was a man of Ionia, on the coast of Anatolia and the islands offshore, and perhaps specifically of Chios.

Ionic and Aeolic had a Greek mainland kinship arising from migrations to Anatolia largely during the Dark Age. The Parian Marble,[23] for whatever value that testimony may have, places the Ionian migration in about 1000 BC. Most migrants probably came from Attica, the district that includes Athens.

Aeolians came, it is thought, from Thessaly and Boeotia. Scholars have noted that Homer's Ionian poetic language contains an undercurrent of Aeolic dialect. Aeolic in Homer's language may be a residue of a much older Aeolian poetic language. How Aeolic entered this Ionian poet's language is uncertain and is a matter of controversy among experts.

3

WHEN HOMER LIVED

When did Homer live? When did alphabetic writing come to Greece? If the answers were known, much else that is mysterious about Homer might be solved. But they are not known, and a mystery remains.

Greece had emerged from the Dark Age, a long period of economic and cultural regression. No one can say how long it lasted. No precise date can be given for its end, but from about 800 BC, there is evidence of new energy, new arts and then literature, expanding into the Classical period. It is difficult to say what the Greeks of the Classical period knew about their distant past. They had, of course, many legends of the past and these they may have accepted as fact. The poet Hesiod, who lived before the Classical period, examined the problem and proposed a Four Age system. That included an Age of Bronze closely linked to an Age of Heroes who lived and fought in the Trojan War. The most recent Age, the age in which Hesiod himself lived, was an Age of Iron which was, according to him, a time of strife and want.[3.1] This scheme, or something similar, and those legends, may have been all that the Classical period Greeks knew, or thought they knew, of the past.

Many of the Classical period thought that Homer lived during the time of the Trojan War. When was the war? What date should be given to Homer? Herodotus (484 BC–425 BC) gave some attention to this. He wrote "I believe that Homer lived no more than 400 years before our time." That would suggest a date around 850 BC.

For those who believed that Homer lived at the time of the Trojan War, that would mean that the war also occurred at about 850 BC. It is clear that Herodotus gives the date as an opinion, and we may see in this a dispute that Herodotus had with other scholars of his time who may have proposed other dates. In short, no one knew when Homer lived, or when the Trojan War occurred.

There are many spurious ancient accounts about Homer. There were biographies such as one by a so-called pseudo Herodotus. There was the claim that an Arctinos of Miletus was a pupil of Homer. His dates would give us Homer's dates with sufficient accuracy, but the dates for Arctinos are inventions. Much of what was written in ancient Greece about Homer, the Trojan War, and much else was invention not fact.

An attempt has been made to date Homer using modern methods, by examining the age of the Homeric language (see Altschuler in Readings). Comparisons were made between cognate words in Homeric Greek, Classical Greek, and Hittite. These are related Indo-European languages and are assumed to have been closely similar in some very ancient time. Original close similarities are assumed to have decreased at a steady rate over time, and that rate can be estimated by comparison of Greek to Hittite. Applying this rate to the differences between Homeric and Classical Greek, a date for Homer can be estimated. That gives a date range of 760–710 BC. However, the validity of such precision by such a method is very doubtful and the date range is equally doubtful.

The time in which Homer lived must be sought through other evidence, implicit evidence, a task heavy with difficulties. The evidence, such as it is, is turbulent, chaotic, like the seas over which Odysseus and his crew sailed, hoping to find their way home. What is wanted is an "absolute" date for Homer, one given by a numerically specific year or narrow range of years. The difficulty in finding an absolute date for Homer is fourfold.

First, and foremost, is the absence of surviving documents other than *Iliad* or *Odyssey* from the time of Homer, or close to that time, that might inform about him.

Second is the absence of a calendar. The Greeks had no year-calendar that extended back well into the age when Homer lived. There was the assumed date of the first Olympiad, the first Olympic games, given as the year 776 BC in our terms. Thereafter, the games were held every four years. One might have said that a certain event concerning Homer happened, for example, during the third Olympiad, and such a reference to an Olympiad would have been sufficiently accurate for the purpose of dating Homer. Unfortunately, there is no such data relating to Homer.

There was a kind of year-calendar relating to Spartan kings, the Spartan king list. It was believed that the list of Spartan kings was known back through the Dark Age. The absolute date of any of these kings was not known, but could be estimated on the basis of three generations of kings per century. Surprisingly, that assumption checks out reasonably well when tested against a list of recent kings. On that assumption, an approximation of the absolute date of Homer might be obtained, but though a date for the Trojan War was supposedly found through this method, it seems that Homer was never dated that way.

Third, there is the archaeological approach and that involves pottery dating. Little remains from the Dark Age and the beginning of Recovery period but pottery, an enduring artifact. In the absence of other means, the archaeologist depends upon pottery design for dates. Pottery designs change over time. A sequence of styles or designs of Athenian pottery has been worked out by archaeologists going back a substantial time before the Classical period. A circumstance relating to Homer might relate to a certain piece of pottery, and thus dated, but that would be at best a relative date, not an absolute date, since the longevity of each pottery style is not known.

And fourth, as if those problems were not enough, there is another pervasive problem. Some words on pre-Classical pottery, some pictures, seem to be taken from *Iliad* or *Odyssey*. The date of this pottery might suggest a date for Homer. However, it seems likely from available evidence that Homer was not the only source, the only poet-singer who told of the Trojan War. The so-called Trojan Cycle deals with the Trojan War and most of these works are probably not by Homer. There may have been tellers of Trojan tales before Homer as well as after. When a reference to the Trojan War is written on a pot, when a reference to the Trojan War is found as an illustration on a pot, though it may sound or look Homeric, it need not have come from Homer or the time of Homer.

With these reservations in mind, the time of Homer is sought.

Looking within *Iliad* and *Odyssey*

Hesiod composed *Works and Days*. This is in part an autobiographical work, and in it he tells of a hard life he lived during bad times. It was difficult to wrest a living from the poor piece of land that he owned, and besides, the judges were corrupt and against him. Yet nowhere in this work is there information that would provide an absolute date for the life of Hesiod. This bodes poorly for the possibility of finding a date for Homer in either *Iliad* or *Odyssey* since Homer does not reveal himself as did Hesiod. There is not a hint of the autobiographical in Homer's works. But something else in *Iliad* or *Odyssey* may provide evidence of the times in which he lived, and composed.

In terms of social customs, material things, political structures that might tell of the times in which Homer lived, *Iliad* and *Odyssey* hint at much, and self-contradict much, and nothing credible can be made from those things. Little enough is known of life in the Dark Age or early Recovery period in Greece against which to judge the time of composition of *Iliad* or *Odyssey*.

In *Iliad*, Homer mentions iron, showing that Homer lived in the Iron Age, but no modern scholar ever doubted that. One of the strangest aspects of *Iliad* is that this work shows no knowledge of writing, strange because there is some reason to believe that writing may have already existed, at least in some parts of Greece, in the time of Homer. Also there is no mention, no hint, of the Dorian invasion in *Iliad*.

Of course, Homer was telling of the long ago Age of Heroes and wanted to preserve authenticity to the extent that he understood it, and therefore ought not to mention writing or Dorians. But surely in a work of the length of *Iliad* there ought to have been one slip-up, one mention of invading Dorians, or of writing. There are certainly other small slip-ups in *Iliad*. But there is no slip-up about writing. There is, however, the mention of "baneful symbols" on a folding tablet in a small story in *Iliad*.[6.1] What are "baneful symbols?" They appear to be something alien to Homer, something that he really did not understand. Mention of baneful symbols does not mean that Homer was aware of writing.

Perhaps Homer did live well before writing in Greece. It remains a possibility. However, it is more likely that, in *Iliad*, Homer was able to maintain a wonderful discipline in which he consciously excluded anachronisms. Anachronisms are obvious in *Odyssey*, however, because Phoenicians are mentioned, out of place in a story assumed to be about the Bronze Age.

In *Odyssey*, Odysseus tells how he took ship with some roving Phoenician traders because he needed transportation to Elis on the west coast of Greece. Phoenicians were people of coastal cities of what today is Syria and Lebanon. At the end of the Bronze Age, around 1200 BC, some of the south coast of Cyprus also was Phoenician as is clear from archaeological evidence. After the Bronze Age, Phoenician ships plied the seas, going ever westward, ever exploring for mineral resources: copper, tin, and gold. As they encountered fixed settlements, there were opportunities for trade. As they pressed westward they encountered Greeks, as Odysseus said, and Greeks became very aware of them.

When was that? Archaeologically based dates are often open to dispute, but it appears that by 900 BC, Phoenicians were in Crete, and a Phoenician temple there is evidence of them. Euboea by the east coast of mainland Greece presents an interesting situation, with evidence of Phoenician jewelry, gold, and much else. That is dated, somewhat uncertainly, to about 900 BC or a bit earlier. Also by about 900 BC there is evidence of them in Sardinia, the Nora Stone with part of a Phoenician inscription. There is evidence of Phoenicians in about 800 BC at what would later be Carthage, and somewhat later in Cadiz, Spain. The Bible reports the trading activity of Hiram, a king of the Phoenician coast of about that time. They are everywhere on the seas.

If Homer lived and composed as early as 900 BC, he would have known of Phoenicians. But so would he have known of them had he lived at a much later date. The Phoenician evidence is an early bound on the date of Homer, and is reasonably consistent with the estimate of Herodotus. Yet most scholars strongly support a much later date for Homer.

Pottery Images

Where there are no written records, archaeologists must depend on other evidence. Greek pottery of many periods have illustrations painted on them and certain pre-Classical pottery seems to illustrate scenes from *Iliad* or *Odyssey*. There are, for example, many images of what seems to be Odysseus and his men driving a stake through the eye of Polyphemus; of horses that may be the Trojan Horse; of heroic deaths perhaps of Hector or Achilles or Patroclus. If the scenes are from the works of Homer, and if the pottery is accurately dated, than the earliest of such illustrations would set a bound on the date in which Homer lived. He would not have lived much earlier than the earliest of such illustrations, and not later.

The problem is that it is likely that many of the stories that are found in *Iliad* or *Odyssey* existed outside of Homer, and even before Homer, sung by earlier poet-singers, and told in folk tales. A modern scholar suggests that in Homer's time there existed in Greece "... ... a great web of vernacular, oral-transmitted mythology ... known to everyone of whatever education and which did not need to depend at all on epic poetry" (see Snodgrass in Readings).

Thus, images on pottery seemingly Homeric could have been inspired by tales that date earlier or later that Homer, and were learned of other than through Homer, and cannot be used to date Homer. In any case, the dates so confidently given for such pottery does not merit confidence as will be discussed further below.

Writing in Greece

It may seem a paradox, but some recent scholars who are the firmest supporters of the orality of *Iliad* and *Odyssey* also maintain that Homer used writing. It seems an inescapable conclusion and will be further considered in Chapter 9. On that assumption, a date for the earliest use of the writing in Greece might cast light on the time in which Homer lived, and worked.

No one doubts that the Greek alphabet came from the Phoenicians. The forms of the Greek letters show that. The names of the letters in Greek reflect that. Herodotus asserts that.

The Phoenician alphabet developed during the Bronze Age in the region where the Northwest Semitic languages were spoken. All around that region, there was writing in cuneiform, a system of hundreds of complex symbols. South of Phoenicia, there was another writing system, also with hundreds of symbols: Egyptian hieroglyphics. Both of these writing systems were sufficiently complex that a professional, the scribe, was required to write or read texts, and this provided good professional employment for centuries in many lands. Alphabetic writing, however, was revolutionary. It had only two dozen or so easily formed symbols, and with this, any man could learn to read and write with no need of a scribe.

Phoenician writing did not include vowels. Yet that did not compromise utility of the system. It was sufficiently functional to fulfill Phoenician needs over hundreds of years. The Hebrew Bible was written with a closely related alphabet without vowels. That did not prevent the writing of the most elevated and varied prose in the Bible. The Phoenician alphabet became a Greek alphabet when vowel symbols were added to the Phoenician consonant symbols.

This was done by using some symbols of the Phoenician alphabet whose sounds were not used in Greek, and these were employed as vowel symbols. With that, the alphabet became an almost ideal system, one in which one basic consonant or vowel would be represented by one written symbol.

Why make a Greek adaptation at all? The Phoenician alphabet, as it was, could probably have been employed for most Greek needs. One need alone suggests itself. Lines of Greek poetic verse could not be written in a system without vowels as this would not meet the needs of dactylic hexameter. The meter could not be represented without vowels. It is perhaps hard to believe and accept the that the Greek alphabet could have been invented for the purpose of recording the works of Homer, or of other poet-singers. It may be easier to understand if it is recognized that such poetic works played a major role in the life of the Greek people.

Where was the Greek alphabet invented? Some Greeks in Cyprus used a syllabic writing system, and held to that stubbornly into the Classical period. It could have been some of those Greeks who developed the Greek alphabetic writing system, for poetic reasons. Greeks and Phoenicians lived side by side in Cyprus since about 1100 BC. Lefkandi on Euboea would be another possibility as it is likely that there had been an enduring Phoenician community there.

The alphabet was "invented" several times over in Greece since there were regional variants of the alphabet in the Greek world. This invention or reinvention might have required no more than that a Greek, seeing the alphabet on a visit to another part of Greece and recognizing its utility, brought home the idea and worked out his own version suitable to his dialect. There is no reason to believe that the alphabet reached all parts of Greece at the same time or even close to the same time.

Date of Writing

That makes the question of when the alphabet arrived in Greece difficult to answer. To say when it arrived in Ionia, the homeland of Homer, is even more difficult. A plausible suggestion was made that writing in Greece required writing material—papyrus. At the time of Egyptian king Psamtik II, a large contingent of Ionian sailors was employed in the Egyptian navy. It would be credible that, on their return, these sailors brought a good supply of papyrus with them which they might be able to sell once back in Ionia. Papyrus is a perfect writing material, used in Egypt and the Middle East for centuries. The date of this venture is a few years after 600 BC. Unfortunately, few believe that Homer lived as late as that date, only a century before the Classical period for, in that case, much more would have been known about him.

Of course, papyrus could have reached Greek shores much earlier. Then there was parchment, a perfectly suitable writing material. And there may have been sheets of lead. Lead has been used as a writing surface, and a story survives that some works of Hesiod were written on sheets of lead. Lead could have been readily available from the silver mines near Athens, as a reduction product of red lead oxide. *Iliad* in present-day print is typically several hundred pages long. A pile of lead sheets sufficient for the writing of *Iliad* in Greek is not credible.

These considerations do not help to date the beginning of Greek writing.

Archilochus

The writings of Archilochus may be helpful. Archilochus was an adventurer, a mercenary soldier, and occasionally a poet. Only some fragments of his poetical work survive. In one, he mentions a "scytale." This is an ancient cypher method, useful in combat, in which one writes on a leather strip wrapped around a stick. Thus, Archilochus knew about writing. Another fragment, dealing with his combat experience, has endeared him to generations.

> *A Thracian mountaineer struts around with my shield. I threw it down by a bush and ran when the fighting got hot. Life seemed more important to me. It was a beautiful shield. To hell with it. I know where I can get another just as beautiful.*

It seems doubtful that anyone but Archilochus himself would have put such verses, some of them personal, and some scathing, into writing. The date of his work is important. Archilochus can be dated with good accuracy to about 652 BC because he mentions king Gyges of Lydia whose dates are known. Gyges' region of activity was not far from Ionia, and it thus appears certain that there was writing in Ionia at this date, and probably earlier.

Papyrus and parchment do not survive decay in the atmosphere of the Greek world, and lead sheets would be a target for metal salvagers. Pottery endures. For that reason, writing occasionally found on pottery becomes important.

The Dipylon Jug

A pottery wine jug, rather beat up over the ages, but no doubt beautiful in its time, was recovered from a site on the outskirts of ancient Athens. This is the so-called Dipylon Jug. Scratched into the surface near the top is Greek alphabetic writing. This writing is somewhat crude but seems to indicate that the jar was meant as a party gift and it says, approximately, "To him that dances the friskiest." The marvel of this writing is that it appears to be in hexameter, the language of the poet-singers and of Homer. The date of manufacture of the Dipylon Jug comes from comparison to similar jugs from nearby Athens.

There had been an excavation in the Agora, the market place of Classical period Athens. Pottery of various ages had been found. By laborious study these have been arranged in a pottery sequence, a series of styles and style changes over time, constituting a kind of time scale. It is to this pottery series that the Dipylon Jug has been compared. From that, the Dipylon Jug has been given a date of 740 BC. The Agora excavators believe that dates in their pottery series have an accuracy of plus or minus 25 years, giving an uncertainty span of 50 years for the Jug.

To the uncertainty of the date of manufacture of the Dipylon Jug is to be added the date of the inscription. There is no reason at all to believe that the alphabetic inscription was applied by the original potter. One would think that a potter would be adverse to scratching his pottery. The writing is probably a post manufacturing affair and could date to decades after the jug was made. This adds even greater uncertainty to the age of this inscription. Thus, the dating of the inscription provides little good information concerning the beginning of writing in Greece.

Nestor's Cup

Nestor, a personality of *Iliad*, was an old warrior, grown old perhaps in years of waiting in front of the walls of Troy for something decisive to happen. He filled the time in spinning yarns, and in drinking, and it is told that no ordinary man could lift his wine cup.

A pottery wine cup of more reasonable size was discovered in Pithekousi, Ishia Italy, and is now called Nestor's Cup. There is a long inscription scratched into the side, in Greek hexameter verse saying, in effect, that the more you drink from this cup the more amorous you will be. Various dates are proposed: Two such dates are 750 BC, and also before 700 BC. All of the cautions expressed about the dating of the Dipylon Jug, and more, apply to dating the inscription on this cup.

There are other examples of early Greek writing, on pottery, pottery sherds, stone. Sources include Italy, Crete, the east coast of Greece, Anatolian Sardis. Dates between 800 BC and 700 BC are given for the most part. Uncertainties in the dates mean that they add no additional information to that given above.

Date of Writing. Date of Homer

The date of introduction of writing in Greece, and in particular in Ionia, is elusive. Historians are left to guess at the date. These cover a large range between 800 BC and 700 BC. The date for Homer is, if possible, even more elusive but the same date range is usually assumed, but certainly not proved.

Thus, a judgment needs to be made. When did Homer live? An acme for Homer just a little earlier than 700 BC seems best. By that time, writing would have been reasonably well established. The time span over which the written *Iliad* would need to survive to the Classical period is less than it would have been for an earlier date. Some of the adventures of Odysseus, written perhaps thirty years after *Iliad*, would match the adventures of the poet Archilochus, about 650 BC.

This somewhat late date for Homer is sometimes denied to him since so little—really nothing—is known about him, and that suggests that he lived in some very remote antiquity. In contrast, something is known of the life of Hesiod, and of Archilochus. However, those poets wrote about themselves. Homer did not, and that might account for the difference.

4

TIME OF THE TROJAN WAR

Iliad and *Odyssey* are the oldest texts we have concerning the Trojan War. Without those, a war at Troy would have no fame, and mention of it by Cypria or other elements of the so-called Homeric Cycle[4.1] would rouse little interest. Though *Iliad* and *Odyssey* are the fundamental sources, the "historicity," of the Trojan War, by which is meant the historic truth of the Trojan War, cannot be found by consulting those texts. It must be found by other evidence using the texts only to point the direction of search.

The first thing that must be acknowledged is that there may not have been a Trojan War, or none of the magnitude and duration of that implied in *Iliad*. There may have been only a raid, a skirmish, tales of which grew over the years of the Dark Age. Yet for the Greek community of Classical times, the Trojan War was an accepted fact. Concerning that the perceptive and critical Greek historian Thucydides seemed to have little doubt. He devoted effort, not to questioning the truth of the war, but to determining why the large Greek army, surrounding Troy and presumably besieging Troy, took ten years to conquer the city. Herodotus did not seriously doubt the war, and consulted the priests in Egypt to confirm it which, apparently, they did to his satisfaction.

When one reads *Iliad*, the immediacy and vividness of the writing lulls one into thinking that it is a factual account. Yet from a reasonable perspective, *Iliad* is a work of fiction, composed in the fertile and brilliant mind of Homer, utilizing stories received from his predecessors, the earlier poet-singers, and probably legends that he may have learned from other sources. This does not mean that there are no valid historic elements in *Iliad*, and it is certainly possible that there was an historic basis for the Trojan War story. Among modern fiction we have Tolstoy's *War and Peace* built around the Napoleonic wars, with many valid historic elements including the war itself. We have *Gone With the Wind*, a work of fiction based on the American Civil War, also with many historical elements. The question then is, was there really a Trojan War as Homer tells, a war on some scale, or was his tale entirely fictional?

What are needed are not legends but historic records, records made at the time and place of the supposed war, or close to the time and place. In what time period should one look, and what place? To answer these questions, several lines of evidence are needed.

Time Period

Hesiod speaks of "Ages" and names a Bronze Age and an Iron Age. Between these, he squeezes in an Age of Heroes. This surely refers to the heroes of the *Iliad* and kindred stories. Homer, with great consistency, speaks of bronze weapons and armor used by his heroes. Thus from *Iliad*:

> *... they dashed their shields together and their spears and the strength of armored men in bronze, and their shields massive in the middle ...*

> *... their eyes were blinded in the dazzle of the bronze light from the glittering helmets ...*

> *... all the plain was filled and shining with bronze of the mortals ...*

... glorious Hector burst in with dark face like sudden night, but he shone with the ghastly glitter of bronze that was girding his skin ...

Extensive use of bronze is confirmed by the findings of archaeology for a time around 1200 BC and before. "Bronze Age" is now used by archaeologists and historians to name a period of the distant past.

It would seem from the frequent mention of bronze that the Trojan War may have taken place in the Bronze Age, the archaeologist's Bronze Age, though the use of bronze armor in that Age was not as extensive as is suggested by Homer's *Iliad*.[4.2] However, that Homer appears to place the War in the Bronze Age does not necessarily make it so historically. The problem is that the ancient story of a conflict at Troy, moving by word of mouth over many

Figure 2. Citadel of Bronze Age Mycenae in artists reconstruction, based on present remains and archaeological evidence. Per Homer, the seat of Agamemnon.

generations through the Dark Age, may have gathered to it stories from various times. Tales of a battle or war at Troy, and memories of bronze-clad warriors, may have had separate origins. The vivid tale of warriors armored in bronze, and a great conflict at Troy as we have it in *Iliad*, could have been a result of merging of once separate story elements at some time in the Dark Age.

It is best, then, to find additional means of dating, at least approximately, the historical conflict we know as the Trojan War.

Mycenae

Because of Homer's skill, the personalities in *Iliad* seem to be part of a legitimate and historical whole. They appear to belong together. Though they are together in the *story*, were they together in *history?* The problem is similar to that above, the distorting effect that can occur over time—the possibility that persons of different periods have been brought together. It has long been suggested that the Greek hero Ajax was of an earlier time than other personalities of *Iliad* because of his body-length shield. That shield is archaeologically more ancient by several hundred years than other weapons or armor in *Iliad*. Likewise, Odysseus seems a person apart, coming from a far-off land, and bringing his own legends. And Achilles, the central figure of *Iliad*, is often hardly evident in the War story as we have it. He sits out much of the story, sulking in his tent. He seems disconnected from the other more southerly Greeks who make up the bulk of the Greek military force in *Iliad*. Thus, all of the pieces so neatly stitched together by Homer need not have been together in the historic sense. And in Chapter 8, it will be shown that oral transmission over the generations can produce just such nonhistoric combinations.

Agamemnon, however, seems to be inseparable from the story of the Trojan War and one could not have an *Iliad* without him. Legend tells that his sister-in-law, Helen, eloped with Paris (Alexander), prince of Troy, while Paris was a guest in the home of Agamemnon's brother Menelaus. To right this wrong, Agamemnon called the warrior power of Greece to arms. It was he who commanded the Greek forces at Troy. It was his quarrel with Achilles that led to the rupture described in *Iliad*. Now, if it is assumed that there was a historical Trojan War, and that Agamemnon was part of it, and if it is further accepted that the citadel of Mycenae belonged to Agamemnon, some further dating is possible.

This great fortress in south-central Greece (Map A), the ruins of which can still be seen, has long been recognized as the site of Mycenae. It appears that there has been a small town there since ancient times just outside this citadel, just as there is today. In ancient times, this town sent troops to fight the Persians and the name and place, Mycenae, was recognized in Classical times. There is no reason to doubt that this is the site of Homer's Mycenae, the seat of Agamemnon's power according to *Iliad*.

Where no writing is found, pottery is the basis for dating. Absolute dates for Mycenae depend on synchronizing pottery findings from Mycenae with certain datable Egyptian artifacts. The dates of Egyptian kings and queens are known with high accuracy. Thus, a Mycenaean Greek pot of the style called Late Helladic IIIB (Late) has been found in the distant Syrian city of Ugarit together with a message written by an official of Egyptian queen Twosert. Her date of rule is known. That date thus dates that pottery, and the pottery dates the stratum at Mycenae in which such pottery was found. This and related correlations provides absolute dates, dates in years, accurate to perhaps a few decades under best conditions, for the Greek pottery sequence associated with Mycenae and other contemporary Greek sites.

Slightly after 1200 BC, a major catastrophe occurred at Mycenae. Buildings were shattered inside and outside the citadel. An olive oil storage facility outside was set ablaze. Other buildings just outside were also destroyed. This was followed by a second period of destruction which was even more damaging than the earlier episode. After that, life in Mycenae seemed to have slipped into a fitful decline into the Dark Age.

If Agamemnon was a real person, king of Mycenae, warrior of the Trojan War, he should be dated to a time earlier than this period of decline and collapse. Thus, in round numbers, he and the Trojan War should be looked for in a time before approximately 1200 BC, toward the end of the Late Bronze Age.

Ancient Scholars

Greek scholars were interested in calculating a date for the Trojan War. Their various calculations are spread over a range of year-dates, but the results largely cluster between 1334 BC and 1126 BC. The basis of their calculations is not clear. Probably most are based on the Spartan king list, a dubious proposition at best. Still, it is strange that this range of dates matches rather closely with the other dates discussed here.

Various lines of evidence, each perhaps weak on their own, converge and support one another. They suggest that if a Trojan War is to be looked for in ancient records, it should be sought before about 1200 BC, and not long before. What ancient records are these? That will be discussed shortly.

Manuel Robbins

The Location of Troy

In the northwest corner of Anatolia (Turkey) is a ruin which since Classical times has been taken to be the site of Homer's Troy. In the ages since the Classical period, the site had been lost. The modern rediscovery of this site is due to Heinrich Schliemann who, in 1870, began excavation of the ruin there based on a recommendation of Frank Calvert, a local resident who thought it to be the site of Troy. Calvert owned some of the land on Hissarlik Hill upon which the ruin is located.

According to Herodotus, Persian king Xerxes after marching north out of Sardis with his army, aiming for a crossing into Europe at the Dardanelles, came to a ruin that he took to be the site of Troy, probably based on local lore. This information would be consistent with the location of Homer's Troy at Hissarlik Hill. Going further back in time, clues from *Iliad* about tides and winds at Troy and the presence of certain islands nearby are also consistent with this location and this ruin as the remains of Troy.

Archaeology has thus far not found any other ruin of the Bronze Age near the west coast of Anatolia which might be Homer's Troy.

The excavated fortress on Hissarlik Hill is modest in size, of oval shape and about 200 meters across. In contrast, the citadel at Mycenae is about 350 meters across and far more impressive with its massive, high, stone walls. At Hissarlik, the ruin is perhaps not so imposing as to impress everyone. R. C. Jebb, a prominent scholar, who wrote as Schliemann completed his excavations, said "the spacious palaces, and wide streets of the Homeric Troy point to a city totally different, both in scale and in character, from anything of which traces exist at Hissarlik."

Jebb expected of the ruins something more grand and glorious. He did not allow for poetic license, for the effect of poet-singers working over generations. Nor was he aware of the lower town outside the stone walls of the citadel but within a wood palisade that would have added to the size of ancient Troy.

There need be no doubt that this site is what Homer knew as Troy. Homer came from Ionia not so far away along the Anatolian coast. It is even possible that he visited this location. The walls would not have been as damaged as now, and the site was probably no longer occupied or only poorly occupied. His imagination, and glorious stories from the past, would supply the rest.

The existence of this site, even in the time of Homer, does not prove that there was a Trojan War. To resolve that, historic records are needed.

5

FROM THE HITTITE RECORDS

For western Anatolia of the Late Bronze Age, what are the historic records? Linear B texts are not helpful. They contain no history. Records which are of this time and place are the Hittite records which have been found in abundance in the Hittite archives at Hattusa, the ancient Hittite capitol in central Anatolia.

It is a remarkable fact that the Hittites of Anatolia were completely lost to history until the beginning of the 20th century, though there were a few obscure references to them in ancient Egyptian records. The Greeks and the Romans, who centuries after the Bronze Age had colonies in Anatolia, appear to have had no knowledge of them. Their disappearance was complete. Yet now, thanks to records which have been discovered in the Hittite archives, Hittite laws, customs, beliefs, history, and the names of Hittite kings, are known far better than are known of many other lands of that time.

Earliest clues to the rediscovery of the Hittites came from Syria where anonymous sculptures and monuments with mysterious writing were found. Then, similar monuments were found in Turkey. A large ruin was found at Bogazkoy, Turkey, east of Ankara and a connection of this site with those monuments was suspected. Excavation at Bogazkoy was begun in 1906 under H. Winckler and, as luck would have it, a vast archive of writing on clay tablets was quickly discovered.

The writing was mostly in the cuneiform characters of Bronze Age Babylon but the language was not Babylonian and was not understood. It was soon discovered that the language, whatever it was, belonged to the Indo-European family of languages. The language is now called Hittite and the people of this writing are called Hittites. Decipherment was aided by the frequent use in these tablets of Babylonian words of known meaning, and decipherment has proceeded continuously to the present time. This site at Bogazkoy was ancient Hattusa, the capital of the Hittite empire.

Figure 3. A carefully executed relief portrait of a Hittite, from the Egyptian Karnak temple.

Those records in the archive that are of the most interest here cover the period of approximately 1400 BC to 1200 BC. They are by no means a complete record of events over that span of time, but they are of outstanding importance. While *Iliad* represents to a large extent lore or legend, filtered through hundreds of years of the illiterate Dark Age in Greece, the Hittite records were inscribed at a time close to the events described and represent true history.

Unfortunately, most tablets are damaged to some degree. Some can be read quite well, others can be read only with difficulty, and yet others are nearly illegible.

Hittites were a relatively small people, especially when compared to populations in Babylonia or Egypt. However, they achieved conquest and power over a vast region from the Aegean Sea in the west, to the upper Euphrates in the east, down through Syria almost to Canaan in the southeast. This was accomplished through consummate skill in diplomacy and military operations in a careful blend. Various small states of Anatolia and Syria were brought into the Hittite orbit as vassal states. The vassal king was required to sign a treaty which bound the vassal in loyalty to the Hittite king. The treaty required that the vassal king support with his armies the Hittites in time of war, return fugitives who had slipped Hittite control, stay within recognized borders, and report events in his region that would be of interest to the Hittite king. There was, of course, the need to send tribute to Hattusa.

The treaty was not one-sided. If the vassal was faithful to his obligations under the treaty, the Hittites would defend him from attack and ensure the succession of his heirs forever. An extensive list of the gods of both sides was attached to the treaty and copies placed in the temples. There, the gods could oversee compliance, be witnesses to violations, and presumably visit punishment on the guilty. It was with the aid of vassal military support that the Hittites were able to extend empire and control over a vast region.

Political Geography

To understand the circumstances or events that are the Trojan War, a map is necessary, a map showing the lands and cities of Western Anatolia toward the end of the Bronze Age. Until the discovery of the archives, knowledge to produce such a map did not exist. The Hittite records give the names of a large number of towns, cities, rivers, mountains, previously unknown to modern scholars, but no map was found. The Hittite archives produce none, and it is doubtful that the Hittites ever used maps. There was not in those times a satisfactory way of determining direction or distance over any large scale and so maps could not be made and probably were not even dreamed of.

Hittite armies moved over large distances to various objectives, and returned successfully. This was accomplished by moving from recognized landmark to landmark. A significant mountain, a lake or river, the sea, a familiar town, a known trail, was all that they needed. These were often named in the Hittite records, but the names are somewhat obscure to us today. Yet these ancient names, these landmarks, are part of what scholars avail of to determine the location of these cities or countries. Comparison of names from the Hittite records to the name of cities or peoples of the coast from Classical or Roman times has also helped.

Seemingly bewildering Anatolian names must be considered. The names of ancient Greek cities and ancient Greek personalities of the Classical period would also seem bewildering, except that we have grown familiar with them through years of exposure to them. They are part of our culture, but not so the names from the Hittite records. Important for understanding historical events relating to Homer's *Iliad* and the Trojan War are the western Anatolian lands known as Seha River Land, Lazpas, Wilusa, Arzawa, Lukka lands, Ahhiyawa, and the cities of Milawata (alternatively called Millawanda) and Apasas. The locations of Wilusa and Ahhiyawa are particularly important. Placing these on a map has not been easy, and has led to much scholarly controversy, but in part for reasons described below the deployment shown in Map C is now widely accepted.

Map C. The political geography of western Anatolia in the Late Bronze Age as reconstructed from various lines of evidence.

The Lukka Land

Hittite records show that the location of the Lukka people were close to the land of Arzawa. Arzawa will be discussed next.

The Hittite records make clear that the Lukka were a turbulent people with only a few towns. No king ruled there. Records from Egypt show that at least once, Lukka people made a piratical raid against Cyprus. These suggest a mountainous location in southwest Anatolia, by the sea. In the Classical period, there was a land called Lycia, (pronounced Lukia) in the southwest corner of Anatolia. It seems likely that the people of Lycia were direct descendants of the Lukka of the Bronze Age. Certain town names of Classical period Lycia approximately match town names of the Lukka as known from the Hittite records. The likelihood that Lycia of the Classical period is the descendent of Lukka of the Bronze Age strongly influences the placement of the Lukka land shown on Map C.

Arzawa

The kingdom of Arzawa was in the west, and near the sea. That is known from Hittite records that tell of the escape by sea of certain Arzawa personalities whom the Hittites were attempting to capture. At various times, Arzawa was sufficiently powerful militarily as to challenge the Hittites for supremacy in Anatolia. This suggests a fairly large population with a good economic base. In the west, that would be found in the agricultural potential of the valleys of the western rivers, primarily the Meander River. Apasas, the capital city of Arzawa, was known to be near the sea. It was known to be near the city of Milawata/Millawanda. These cities of the Late Bronze Age, Apasas and Milawata, can be equated with

Classical period Ephesus and Miletus. These considerations place Arzawa on the map as shown.

Seha River Land

This country was a kingdom of modest size. As Arzawa and Seha River Land were once members of a close political alliance, the kingdom of Seha River Land, as the Hittites called it, must have been near Arzawa. Further, there was the so-called Manapa-Tarhunda Letter. Manapa-Tarhunda was king of Seha River Land and a Hittite vassal. (Anatolian personalities mentioned here and later are summarized in Appendix B). This letter will be discussed further in Chapter 7, but here it is sufficient to note that Manapa-Tarhunda was reporting local events to the Hittite king as required of him by his vassal treaty. He mentions fugitives and the island of Lazpas. That means he is near Lazpas. Lazpas is equated with the island of Lesbos as known in Classical Greek times. That places Seha River Land near the sea, and just north of Arzawa.

Classical Period Names

The beginning of the Greek Classical period was approximately seven hundred years after the Hittite records were written. In the intervening time, Greek high culture collapsed and Greece descended into the Dark Age. The Hittites in Anatolia disappeared without a trace. Yet the Greeks of the Classical period were familiar with Lycia, a region in south western Anatolia. They knew of a city on the coast called Miletus. They knew of a city, Ephesus. They knew of an island northward along the coast called Lesbos. These must be what in the Bronze Age were called Lukka, Milawata, Apasas, Lazpas.

These equations, shown in Appendix C, are remarkable. When allowances are made for spelling differences between Luvian and Greek, and between the Bronze Age and the Classical period, they suggest a continuity of settlement in these sites from the Bronze Age to the Classical period. The tie between these Classical period names and Bronze Age names ratify the placements as shown on the Map.

Wilusa

From the records, it is clear that Wilusa is a land in the Anatolian west. Indeed, it is a land central to the problem of the Trojan War. The Manapa-Tarhunda Letter refers to Wilusa as it does Lazpas. As Lazpas/Lesbos is an island just offshore, logic places Wilusa nearby and by the sea, and north of Seha River Land.

For Homer, Ilios and Troy are synonyms. Both names are used in *Iliad* to refer to the city, and the name "*Iliad*" comes from the name Ilios. There is good reason to believe that the spoken Greek of Ionia and of Homer had once contained the "w" sound, written as a Greek letter known as a "digamma." It was later dropped from writing, probably reflecting a disappearance from the spoken language of Ionia. It seemed very likely, at least too many scholars, that the original form of Ilios had once had an initial "w" sound and was thus Wilios. It is but a step to equate Greek Wilios with Wilusa of the Hittite records.

What of the name Troy? There is a Hittite text that tells of a confederation of small states in northwestern Anatolia that existed many years before the record was written. It is called the Assuwa Confederation. Two members of the Confederation were Wilusiya, an early spelling of Wilusa, and Taruisa. This last has impressed many as likely an early reference to Troy.

If this interpretation is correct, then the Hittite texts preserve the names Ilios and Troy. It is likely that Wilusa refers to a country and Taruisa to a city (or perhaps the other way around), and it would be understandable that by the time of Homer many centuries later, this distinction would not have been remembered.

The ruin at Hissarlik Hill is located in the midst of what Map C shows as Bronze Age Wilusa, and scenic descriptions in *Iliad* are fully compatible with a location of Homer's Ilios-Troy in Bronze Age Wilusa.

There is more evidence that supports the identity of Wilusa with the Ilios-Troy of Homer.

Alaksandus

Hittite king Muwatalli II (see Appendix A) knew early in his reign that there would be a final showdown between the Hittites and the Egyptians. There had long been friction between them concerning vassal states in Syria. A great battle did take place, the famous Battle of Kadesh. Anticipating the oncoming conflict, Muwatalli took all necessary steps to stabilize his western region. Uprisings in the west, while the Hittite army was far away in Syria in the southeast, were not to be tolerated.

Muwatalli made sure that vassal treaties in the west were updated, and that reliable kings were on the thrones of these states. He confirmed Alaksandus as king of Wilusa. That was made official by what is called the Alaksandus Treaty. The find of the tablets upon which this treaty is written is one of the most fortunate in Hittite archaeology.

This name was a striking thing. As early as 1911, D. D. Luckenbill of the University of Chicago, believed that he recognized in the name Alaksandus, the Greek name Alexandros, prince of Troy. This equation is now accepted by most scholars. It can be supposed, among several possibilities, that the Hittite king had a Greek, Alaksandus or Alexandros, in his service and placed him on the throne of Wilusa. A loyal man in time of need. That such can occur is shown by a text of generations later in which Hittite King Tudhaliya IV (1239 BC–1209 BC) wrote that he intended to place a certain Walmu on the throne of Wilusa. Hittites might place kings on the thrones of vassal states if the throne was vacant or if the present king was for some reason not up to the job. That Alaksandus is a king, but Alexandros of *Iliad* is a prince, is not a serious objection. That a royal personage of Wilusa of the Bronze Age appears in Homer's *Iliad* as Alexander appears to confirm that Wilusa is Ilios, Troy.[5.1]

Appaliuna

A long list of gods of both sides was inscribed as witnesses in Hittite vassal treaties. The list was similar, treaty to treaty. In the Alaksandus Treaty, however, one interesting god stands out in the list of witnesses and that is Appaliuna. There is some damage at the first letter, but this spelling is widely accepted. The name appears in no other treaty known from the archives.

In *Iliad*, the god Apollo is written as Apollon. According to legend, Apollo helped build the walls of Troy. A priest of Apollo had a shrine nearby Troy according to *Iliad*, and there was an Apollo shrine within the city. Apollo descended from Olympus in a rage and came down to the Greek camp and launched the arrows of plague at the Greeks. Greek funeral fires burned night and day.

Later, he joined the battle on the side of Troy. As *Iliad* notes about Apollo-

> *the god grim set on victory for the Trojans ...*

The case seems clear, and Homer understood, Apollo was originally a Trojan god.

Apollo was a late arrival in the Greek family of gods. The Linear B records testify to many gods of Bronze Age Greece. Apollo is not among them. It appears that Apollo originally came from Troy, just as Aphrodite came from Cyprus. The process by which foreign gods entered the Greek pantheon is unknown. It is enough here to note that Apollo's apparent appearance in a treaty relating to Wilusa strongly supports the view that Wilusa was Homer's Troy.

Ahhiyawa

Ahhiyawa has not yet been placed on Map C. The location of Ahhiyawa is at the center of the greatest and still running controversy since the earliest translations of the Hittite texts. Many scholars firmly believe, and others firmly deny, that the reference is to Greece. Linguistic and historic considerations are involved.

Linguistic

The dispute started almost immediately after Emil Forrer, a Swiss scholar, in 1924 claimed to have found Greeks in the Hittite records. It starts with a term, "Achaean." In *Iliad*, Achaean (Homer's "Achaioi") refers to the Greeks. In the Hittite records, there was frequent mention of a land called Ahhiya or Ahhiya-wa.

Was this not a Hittite reference to the Achaioi, the Greeks? Thus the equation

Ahhiyawa=Achaioi.

That Ahhiyawa refers to a place while Achaioi refers to a people is not, of itself, an obstacle to the equation. Linguistically trained scholars quickly declared that Forrer was mistaken and the equation was impossible. In short order, other scholars began to propose hypothetical intermediate words (X) that made the equation Ahhiyawa=X=Achaioi possible. Many such intermediate words have been proposed over the years. With many possibilities for that intermediate word, it could be that one was correct, and that the Ahiyawa means the Greeks. Yet none of the intermediate words could be proven, nor disproven.[5.2] The present situation is that Ahhyawa=Achaioi cannot be used as proof, though it may be true that the Hittites were referring to Greeks. That proof, if it exists, must come from historical considerations.

Historical Data

In the Bronze Age, there was a term used in diplomatic letters, "Great King." It signified a king over other kings, or rarely a sovereign king not subordinate to other kings. The clear implication was that a Great King had substantial political, military, and economic power at his disposal. Kings of Egypt, Babylon, Assyria, and Mittani were addressed as Great King. Great Kings were allowed to address one another as "My Brother." It would be unthinkable for a Great King to address a lesser king with this term, and certainly a lesser king could not address a Great King as My Brother.

At an earlier time, Assyria was a small power. Her king had no exalted address. Then, the Assyrians made some significant conquests in the direction of the Hittite land and thus gained an elevated status. With little delay, the Assyrian king wrote to the Hittite king and demanded that he now be addressed as Great King and My Brother. This threw the Hittite king into a depression and he replied, "Don't write to me any more about Great King and Brother."

Great King and the Tawagalawas Letter

The Tawagalawas Letter from Hittite King Hattusili III (1264 BC–1239 BC) to the king of Ahhiyawa is the most important text from the Hittite archives dealing with Ahhiyawa. The purpose was to do something about Piyama-Radu (see Appendix B).

Piyama-Radu was a native of the west coast. He had no obvious formal position anywhere. But he was a skilled political operator, military adventurer, and provocateur. He worked against Hittite interests in many places in the west over many years. In some way, how is not clear how, he was affiliated with the king of Ahhiyawa. At about the time of the letter, the Hittites were closing in on him and he had taken refuge with Ahhiyawa. The entire purpose of the letter was to implore that the king of Ahhiyawa put an end to Piyama-Radu's activities.

This letter will be examined further in Chapter 7. In the letter, three times Hattusili addresses the king of Ahhiyawa as "Great King." The first tablet or page of this letter has not been found, and there the salutation would be expected to contain even more references to Great King. Hattusili also refers to the king of Ahhiyawa as "My Brother" over two dozen times. He mentions an earlier letter from the king of Ahhiyawa to the Hittites in which the Hittite king is called My Brother. From the use of these terms it cannot be clearer. The Hittites recognized that Ahhiyawa was a significant power, with most or all the attributes associated with such power. Where in Anatolia can this land be found? An examination of evidence dealing with western Anatolia is revealing.

In the northwest corner of Anatolia there was in earlier years a league of states called the Assuwa Confederation, mentioned earlier. A conflict with the Hittites brought the Hittite army and they destroyed the Assuwa Confederation. There may have been some Greeks involved in the battle as mercenaries on the side of Assuwa. A Greek sword, taken as booty, was found in the ruins of the Hittite capital, Hattusa.

The countries belonging to the Confederation were listed by name on a tablet (a few names are illegible). There was no land called Ahhiyawa among them, nor does any subsequent history of the northwest of Anatolia show any such state.

What about the center? In the center-west of Anatolia, there was Arzawa. That powerful country had at one time challenged the Hittites for supremacy in Anatolia. Based on what he chose to consider a provocation, Hittite King Mursili II (1321 BC–1295 BC) marched west with the largest army the Hittites had yet assembled in the west and campaigned there for two years. Hittite forces reached the Aegean Sea. Arzawa was destroyed as an independent state. Her king, Uhha-Ziti, fled "to the islands." A son took ship to Ahhiyawa. There was no hint anywhere, in all the movements of the Hittite army through central western Anatolia, of any state called Ahhiyawa.

Perhaps Ahhiyawa was in the southwest. In the southwest of Anatolia, in the time of Hittite King Tudhaliya II (1390 BC–1370

BC), there was a minor Hittite vassal named Madduwatta, a good Luvian name. His area of operation was somewhere near the northern edge of Lukka Lands or near the headwaters of the Meander River. His story, found in the Hittite archives, is one of the most fascinating tales of an ambitious personality to be found anywhere. He was attacked by a certain Attarissiyas, and a Hittite military detachment twice came and saved him. Attarissiyas had 100 or more chariots with him and probably hundreds of infantry. This Attarissiyas is referred to as a "man of Ahhiya," an early form of the word Ahhiyawa. This is the earliest known reference in the Hittite archives to Ahhiyawa. Chariot forces are ordinarily not stationed in open country. The most likely place to have served as a base for Attarissiyas would have been Milawata (Miletus).

Nowhere in the record of Hittite military operations concerning Madduwatta and Attarissiyas in the southwest of Anatolia, is a country of Ahhiyawa evident. It cannot be Milawata which hardly then, or ever, could be considered a powerful state. Indeed, the Hittites entered Milawata under Hitttite king Mursili II (1321 BC–1295 BC) and destroyed it, an event confirmed by archaeological evidence. It was rebuilt.

If Ahhiyawa was a powerful state, the realm of a Great King, and if it was located in Anatolia, there would have been some record of a military clash at some time between the Hittites and Ahhiyawa. There is no such clash mentioned in the records. Thus, in spite of Hittite marches over all of western Anatolia, north, center, and south, there was no state of Ahhiyawa to be found. Ahhiyawa cannot be placed on the map of Anatolia.

Where Was Ahhiyawa?

It is necessary to look further westward. No island of the Aegean Sea had more than a harbor settlement, or at most a few towns. None of the islands could be Ahhiyawa, the seat of a Great King. Further west, across the Aegean Sea, there is mainland Greece. Here, there was the obviously powerful Mycenae. There was Tiryns nearby. To the west on the mainland was the palace at Pylos, and to the north there were Thebes, Orchomenus, and Gla. Any confederation of these kingdoms under one king would certainly qualify as the domain of a Great King. In the absence of Greek historical texts of the Bronze Age, it is not possible to confirm that political arrangement, but it is clear that these centers at least shared a common culture. Though *Iliad* is not a history book, it is possible that it correctly recalls one Great King over the Greeks of that time.

Based on archaeological evidence, primarily pottery, Greeks had been trading and living at places along the Anatolian coast and the offshore islands over many years. The Hittites certainly must have known of the Greeks, and it is very reasonable to expect that they would know of the situation of mainland Greece. What did they call this land and these people? There is no term anywhere in the Hittite records that matches the need, except the term Ahhiyawa.[5.3]

Ahhiyawa must be accepted as the Hittite term for the land of the Greeks, and people of Greek ethnicity. Most scholars now accept this. Here, from this point forward, the term "Greek" will be used instead of Ahhiyawa or people of Ahhiyawa.

With this assumption, it is interesting to note two Greeks by name. Attarissiyas, the "man of Ahhiya," is the first. Some see in this name a short form of the Greek name Atreus, father of Agamemnon and Menelaus of *Iliad*. This does not mean that Attarissiyas is the person implied in *Iliad*, only that the name is the same. The second is Tawagalawas, mentioned in the letter of that name. He is the brother of the Greek king. The name is taken to be Greek Ete(w)okle(w)es and thus, once the old-fashioned digammas are dropped, the good Greek name Eteocles. These would be the earliest Greeks known to history, and the earliest known Greek names.

6

OPPORTUNITY AND ADVENTURE

The Hittites were a land power, and Hittite interests and ambitions were largely directed landward, for the most part southeast toward Syria. The Greeks, in contrast, were primarily a sea power. By the end of the Bronze Age, they had occupied Crete and probably southern Italy. Not long after the close of the Bronze Age they had colonized part of Cyprus. The close-to-home coast of Anatolia across the Aegean Sea was not ignored.

There are stories and legends, probably from the Bronze Age. Bellerophon was a Greek from Argos who was exiled to the Lukka Land in Anatolia across the Aegean Sea. There, he vanquished the fire-breathing monster and was given the king's daughter in marriage.[6.1] In a different story, a heroic team of Argonauts sailed into the Aegean, along the Anatolian coast past Troy, into the Dardanelles and the Black Sea. Their adventures were told and retold by the Greeks. Greeks attacked Seha River Land and Troy according to Cypria. More about that in the next chapter.

There is more than legend. From the Hittite archive, there is an interesting letter from a king of Greece to the king of the Hittites. This letter is substantially damaged, but scholars have given it a plausible reading.

In the letter, the Greek king refers to one of his ancestors, perhaps his grandfather or great-grandfather. That earlier king had a close alliance with the king of Assuwa, of the Assuwa Confederation in western Anatolia. That was long ago, before the confederation

Looking for Homer

was destroyed in a war with the Hittites. The Assuwa king had given his daughter in marriage to that earlier Greek king and had also given some offshore islands to that Greek king, as a dowry perhaps.[6.2] The close relationship of the Greeks with Assuwa is clear enough. Very likely, certain Greeks fought alongside the men of Assuwa in the war against the Hittites. Recall the Greek sword of that time taken back to the Hittite capital Hattusa and dedicated to the Storm God.

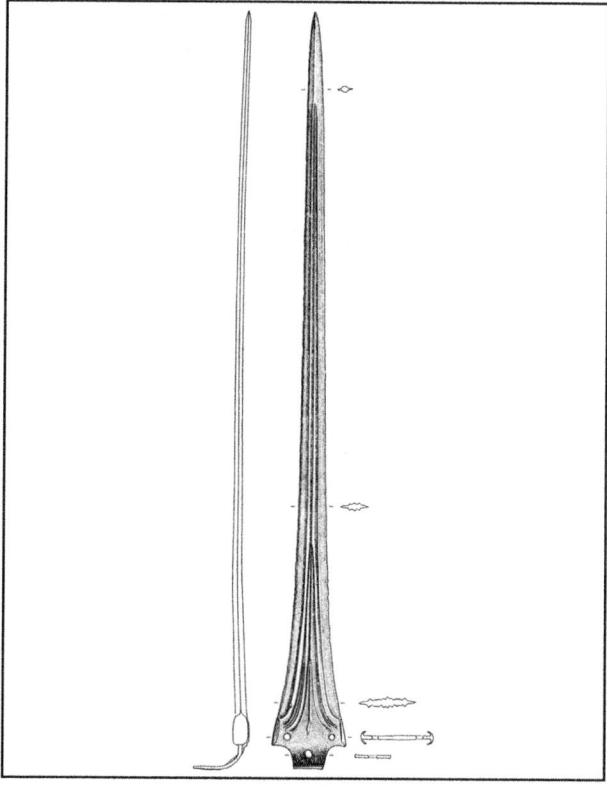

Figure 4. Greek sword found by archaeologists at Hattusa. It is inscribed "As Great King Tudhaliya smashed the Assuwa country he dedicated this sword to the Storm God."

Now, at the time of this letter, the country of Assuwa was in the distant past. The present king of the Greeks wants an assurance from the king of the Hittites that he, the Hittite king, recognizes the legitimacy of the Greek claim to the islands. The argument would be, in present-day terms, that Assuwa was a recognized and legitimate state at the time the gift was made. And therefore the gift was legitimate then, and remains legitimate. It is clear enough. At an early date, the Greeks had a presence on the west coast of Anatolia.

For the Greeks, the Aegean Sea was virtually a Greek lake. This Sea is bound on the west and north by mainland Greece, on the east by Anatolia, and by Crete on the south. For the time period of interest here, approximately 1400 BC to 1200 BC, there is archeological evidence of the presence of Greeks on the Anatolian coasts and islands.

Due to the passage of time, little physical evidence remains. It is to be expected that not every Greek Bronze Age settlement of coastal Anatolia or the islands has been found, or excavated. Further, there may be evidence under present-day towns but it is not possible to excavate there. Particularly for archaeological work done before World War II, evidence has been poorly reported or the evidence itself has been lost. Pottery or pottery fragments provide important information, but these are rarely found. Greeks of the Bronze Age would have settled in river valleys of the Anatolian coast where boats could be moored and the good soil farmed. Over the millennia since the Bronze Age, riverine floods might have washed away pottery or other evidence of occupation.

Pottery evidence is all important. Time period or date of Greek pottery is told by the pottery shape and painted decoration. Style changed over the years in a way that archeologists recognize, and to which dates have been assigned. For the time period of interest here, the pottery is called Late Helladic, abbreviated LH, and the following date ranges have been assigned:

LH IIIA1=from 1420 BC to 1380 BC
LH IIIA2=from 1380 BC to 1310 BC
LH IIIB=from 1310 BC to 1190 BC
LH IIIC=from 1190 to 1050 BC

These dates, broad as they are, are approximate, but is the best that can be done for such remote times.[7,6] The results of archaeological investigation, using pottery to identify the period, are summarized below.

Miletus

Miletus is the most significant site of Greek activity along the Anatolian coast. Before the Greeks came, it was a Minoan (Cretan) settlement. Historians speak of a Thalassocracy, in which Minoans ruled the seas and established outposts in various places in the Aegean and eastern Mediterranean. Then the Greeks came and took over these sites. They occupied the Minoan capital of Knossos. In Miletus, the Greek infiltration appears to have begun even before 1400 BC.

Attarissiyas, the "man from Ahhiya," a Greek, has already been mentioned. He probably operated from a base in Miletus. That would have been in the time of Hittite King Tudhaliya II, around 1370 BC. Archaeologists have found Greek style kilns of this period in Miletus, and remains of LH IIIA2 Greek pottery. A Greek pottery figurine, such as may have been used for religious purposes, was also found.

Hittite records suggest that Uhha-Ziti (1318 BC), the king of neighboring Arzawa, had stirred up trouble by urging that Miletus revolt against the Hittites, and that suggests that Miletus was then under some form of Hittite control. If Uhha-Ziti did that, it was a big mistake. The Hittites came and destroyed Arzawa and chased Uhha-Ziti off to one of the islands and a son off to Ahhiyawa, to the Greeks. Archaeologists have found that Miletus was destroyed by fire, perhaps at that time. They think that the destruction was purposeful, the result of conflict. At some time later, a major defensive wall was built around the city. A cemetery has been excavated bearing remains of Greek pottery with LH IIIB designs. Another Greek religious figurine was found, and Greek-style chamber tombs were also found. The tombs would be dated to just after 1300 BC. Excavators believe that an even earlier use was made of the cemetery, perhaps back to Minoan times. The existence of Greek pottery, figurines, and Greek tombs is a nearly certain indicator of the presence of Greeks.

There is no doubt that Miletus was the major Greek enclave in western Anatolia, but like other sites, it contained a mixed Greek and non-Greek population.

Other Sites

Along the western shore of Anatolia or near it, cities or settlements at Ephesus, Clazomenae, and Colophon show Greek pottery. Pottery of periods LH III A and B are represented. In Troy, there was LH IIIA2 pottery, and more of later types.

On the islands offshore, there is a similar story—remains of Bronze Age Greek pottery. In Rhodes, there is extensive evidence of LH IIIA2 pottery and later, Greek tombs. Further north along the coast, the islands of Chios, Lesbos, and Lemnos show Bronze Age Greek pottery.

Not all pottery evidence proves a Greek presence, of course. The pottery could have arrived in trade, or even have been manufactured locally in Greek style, to meet a local demand. But neither is a Greek presence at these localities ruled out. The absence of Greek pottery does not mean that Greeks were not there. Greek pottery was a luxury ware. Not all Greeks who settled in western Anatolia need have required it, or afforded it, and as a practical matter, they could have made do nicely with locally made Anatolian ware. Archaeologists have had a tendency to ignore Anatolian pottery when found. Anatolian pottery had low esthetic value, and did not provide interest in things Greek which those archaeologists may have developed during their own Classical studies.

Greek records of Mycenaean times, the Late Bronze Age, also offer evidence of Greek activities along Anatolian shores. Certain Linear B tablets contain the names of working women. They were likely indentured or slaves, and the existence of slavery in the Bronze Age is certain. It is clear that women played an important role in the Mycenaean economy, employed, probably in large numbers, in weaving and other crafts. Some of their names reveal their origin. Thus, in present-day terms, if a woman was referred to as the "Parisian," it would be evident that she was from Paris. From the Linear B tablets from Pylos, by such personal names the Anatolian localities of Knidos, Miletus, Chios, seem to be referred to.

Thus, as is shown by a variety of evidence, Greeks, perhaps as traders, perhaps as adventurers or settlers, were present along the Anatolian west coast. If a soldier of fortune, an adventurer, a

Greek or an Anatolian wished to organize raids, piratical attacks, invasions along the coast of Anatolia, he could find Greeks enough who might go along with him. Or, raiders could easily come from mainland Greece. In these circumstances, Troy might well see to her walls in expectation of trouble.

7

THE WAR AT TROY

Herodotus struggled to find true history. He asked the priests of Egypt if Helen and Menelaus visited Egypt as reported in *Odyssey*. Herodotus thought of the Trojan War as so important that the Egyptians would know of it, a war he had dated to 400 years before his time, in a barbaric land far from Egypt. Such is the effect of ethnocentrism.

Whatever the historic basis of the Trojan War story, it is certain that the scope of the conflict had grown in the retelling by Greek poet-singers over the many generations of the Dark Age. Thus, if the Trojan War is to be found in Hittite records, it should not be expected that those records would reflect the size and duration of the War as told in *Iliad*. There will be no thousands of Greek warriors in shining armor, no stories of knightly combat and heroic valor. Hittite records are notoriously antiseptic. The bureaucratic scribes in far-off Hattusa who made the records and archived them had not an ounce of poetry in them.

Piyama-Radu

The events described here occurred during the reigns of Hittite kings Mursili, Muwatalli, and Hattusili (see Appendix A). From the Hittite archives, one treaty and two letters are important. These have been mentioned in Chapter 5.

The so-called Alaksandus Treaty was the work of Muwatalli (1295 BC–1271 BC). It pledged that the Hittites would send troops to defend Wilusa (Troy) should it be attacked.

Somewhat later in date is the Manapa-Tarhunda Letter. Manapa-Tarhunda was king of Seha River Land and was a Hittite vassal. In this letter, he reported to Hittite king Muwatalli. A dire situation has arisen in Seha River Land. Piyama-Radu is there.

Still later is the Tawagalawas Letter[7.1] that may be dated to the time of King Hattusili III (1264 BC–1239 BC). In this long and somewhat rambling letter, Hattusili wrote to the Greek king. Piyama-Radu must be stopped and his activities suppressed.

Who was Piyama-Radu? Though his name is Anatolian, he was in some way allied with the Greeks and employed by them. His son-in-law, Atpas, was governor of the Greek enclave of Miletus.

The activities of Piyama-Radu reflect an enduring Greek aggressiveness and opportunism along the west coast of Anatolia. The employment of this non-Greek had advantages for the Greeks. Piyama-Radu knew the territory, and he spoke the Luvian language of the west coast. He could perhaps draw away some of the petty kings in the west from allegiance to the Hittites. He knew where military advantages may be gained at low risk. And his activities afford the Greeks a certain diplomatic "deniability." He could be cut loose or given up if necessary, if Hittite hostility became too great. The Greeks could not afford to lose Miletus, their firm enclave in western Anatolia, to an angry Hittite king and an aroused Hittite army.

The records show that Piyama-Radu attacked Hittites or Hittite allies on numerous occasions. Writing to the Greek king in the Tawagalawas Letter, Hattusili asked:

> *Piyama-Radu keeps attacking my territory. Does My Brother know of this or does he not?*

Well, of course he does. By putting this as a question rather than an accusation, Hattusili was allowing the Greek king some deniability.

Seha River Land was located along the valley of the Kaikos River, as the Greeks of the Classical period called it. And just offshore was the island of Lazpas (Lesbos). Manapa-Tarhunda of Seha River Land was beset by troubles. He wrote to the Hittite king as follows:

> *My sickness is terrible and beats me down. General Kassu has arrived and brought along the Hittite troops. [... blank] set out for Wilusa to attack [... blank]. ... Piyama-Radu is here and has humiliated me. He has set Atpas over me. He has attacked Lesbos ...*

That is the essential part of the letter. The rest is concerned with the loss of skilled workers who have gone over to Piyama-Radu and Atpas.[7.2]

This letter requires a reasonable interpretation consistent with events of those times. Piyama-Radu has invaded Seha River Land and installed his son-in-law, Atpas, as defacto ruler. He then moved against Lesbos and subdued it. These are obvious stepping stones to Troy, and Troy is the next target. He has done this with the Greeks, for whom he is a front-man and agent. The Greeks provided ships and men. The Hittites knew of this. They detested Piyama-Radu and intend to stop him. They knew from experience of encroachments in western Anatolia by the Greeks, and that was a deep concern. The Hittites sent an army through Seha River Land and on to Troy, in response to treaty obligations, to oppose the move by Piyama-Radu and the Greeks.

This interpretation is supported by what king Hattusili further said in the Tawagalawas Letter, written a few years after the events described in the Manapa-Tarhunda Letter. Since those events, the Hittite and Greek kings had come to some understanding. Diplomacy prevailed, but Piyama-Radu was still a problem for the Hittites. Now Hattusili urges the Greek king to say the following to Piyama-Radu:

> *Concerning the matter of Wilusa* [Troy] *about which we* [Greeks and Hittites] *were at enmity, we have made peace.*

This remarkable letter confirms that the Greeks were with Piyama-Radu in the attack on Troy.[7.3] This attack led to conflict with the Hittites, which ultimately was resolved. Again, the Greeks had to judge their risks. As noted earlier, they could not risk the loss of Miletus, their main base in western Anatolia. As for Piyama-Radu, the wife of Hattusili, Queen Pudu-Hepa, wrote to a certain ruler (in a now fragmented letter):

> *If you seize Piyama-Radu I will send you a bird of gold (and other objects of gold).*

Piyama-Radu was even offered a vassal position by Hattusili, if that would quiet him, but Piyama-Radu was suspicious. No one knows his end.[7.4]

These events may be taken as the historic basis of the story of the Trojan War. More details could not be expected of the Hittite records. While the story of the Trojan War loomed large in the minds of the ancient Greeks, and by cultural inheritance in the

Figure 5. Part of figure that stands guard at an entrance gate to the strong-walled city of Hattusa. Through this gate, a road leads to a chamber containing Hittite archives.

modern world, the events were to the Hittites just one of many other serious problems of that time with which they had to deal. What is remarkable, however, is how closely the matter just described matches what the Greeks say of the Trojan War.

The Greeks Speak

It may seem implausible to anyone steeped in the Homeric tradition to believe that an attack on Troy started with an attack on Seha River Land. About this, it is best to consult the Greeks.

Cypria was one of the works that the Greeks of the Classical period had which told about the war at Troy. Cypria had been attributed to Homer, along with several other poetic works dealing with the War. It tells that Greek forces under Agamemnon gathered at Aulis. Under the navigational command of Achilles, the force set sail for Troy. They made their landing on the Anatolian shore and immediately engaged the defending forces. It was a bloody affair with casualties on both sides. Then, the Greeks made a startling discovery. They were not at Troy at all. They had landed at Mysia. They had been fighting against Mysians all that time. They corrected themselves and later proceeded to Troy.

What was Mysia? It was what in the Bronze Age the Hittites called Seha River Land. No one knows what the Greeks of the Bronze Age called this region. By the time of the Classical period in Greece, and certainly earlier, the region was called Mysia, or alternatively Teuthrania. Cypria reports that, in Bronze Age terms, the Greeks had landed in Seha River Land and fought there, and then proceeded to Troy (see Appendix D).

As Cypria is known only from late texts, it might be thought that this story is a late invention, even later than the Classical period. But this story from Cypria is supported by the early poet and soldier Archilocus (652 BC) who wrote of it (see Appendix E). From the Greek poet Pindar (500 BC) it is learned that Agamemnon and Menelaus fought alongside Achilles in Mysia, just as Archilochus and Cypria say. Cypria itself had the highest reputation among the

Greeks in the Classical period, and more stories were taken from it by vase painters and playwrights than from Homer's *Iliad*.

There is nothing in *Iliad* that contradicts what is said in Cypria. *Iliad* is silent about the landing at Troy, but does say that Achilles attacked and conquered Lesbos.[7,5] And *Odyssey* says that the Greeks attacked Mysia.

The Greek testimony is a remarkable corroboration of the evidence from Hittite records of the Bronze Age. It appears that the historic background of the Trojan War is found in the Hittite records of the time of Hittite kings Muwatalli and Hattusili.

Archaeology at Hissarlik Hill

What, if anything, can archaeology say about an attack on Troy? The ruin at Hissarlik Hill is that of Homer's Troy. That much was pronounced to the wide world by Heinrich Schliemann. He excavated there, off and on, from 1870 to 1890.

Schliemann, who dug rather haphazardly, found himself over his head, both physically and figuratively. He was wise enough to bring in architect Wilhelm Dorpfeld, who brought much-needed order and discipline to the excavation work. Dorpfeld was in charge in 1893 and 1894. An archaeological team headed by Carl Blegen of the University of Cincinnati worked at Hissarlik from 1932 to 1938. In 1988, a large excavation team headed by Manfred Korfmann of Tubingin University began new work. They have meticulously reexamined the old work and extended it. To them belongs particular credit for discovering the "lower town" that existed just outside of the walls of the citadel on the south side.

It has been known since the work of Dorpfeld that there were two incidences of destruction at Troy in the Late Bronze Age. Since Dorpfeld's discovery, scholars have taken for granted that one destruction, or the other, was a consequence of the Trojan War.

As in all ancient cities, each construction phase was built over the remains of the previous phase, one on top of another. Troy was very ancient with several building phases. The phase of concern here is usually referred to as Troy VI. It is the citadel of Troy VI, with its buildings and enclosing stone walls, that has had much of the attention. Outside, in the lower town, there must have been dwellings, but evidence of them has long since eroded away.

There is good evidence that a major catastrophe struck Troy VI. Part of the citadel wall was thrust down. Buildings within the citadel collapsed. There was charred wood, indicating fire. Blegen stated that he saw no overt evidence of war, and that the catastrophe must have been the result of an earthquake. The region is known to be earthquake-prone. Whether of earthquake or war is a matter of judgment.

The date of that destruction presents problems as the date depends on pottery evidence, on the few broken pieces of Greek vases found in the ruins. Blegen reported that the pottery belonged primarily to pottery phase LH IIIA2, with a small amount of LH IIIB. In years, that might be approximately 1290 BC or a little later. Others, perhaps more expert in the matter, who have examined the pottery, place the date close to 1250 BC. A conclusion that may be drawn is that no precise date can be provided by pottery for the destruction of Troy VI.[7.6]

Evidence indicates that the walls were quickly restored. Within the citadel, restoration appeared to have been hasty, and much space was converted to food storage. It seems, somehow, a much poorer city. Archaeologists noted no evidence of any cultural or ethnic change, however, and assume the same people lived in the post-destruction time as in the previous time. This new period is designated Troy VIIa.

Troy VIIa was then struck by a catastrophe even greater than the earlier one. There is extensive evidence of fire, and some evidence of dead bodies. This suggests to some that the destruction was the result of war. Yet that need not be so. An accidental fire on a day in which a strong wind was blowing off the Dardanelles, would produce the same results.

The date of this second destruction has led to controversy. Blegen believed that he had found some LH IIIA pottery fragments but mostly LH IIIB in the ruins. He stated that he found no pottery which was surely of LH IIIC style. Others who have looked at that pottery see some LH IIIC and no LH IIIA. More to the point, the archaeologists of the Tubingin excavation definitely found LH IIIC pottery in the ruins. That would produce a destruction date after about 1200 BC, and some estimates even place the date as late as about 1150 BC. As with the date of the earlier destruction, a precise date of destruction of Troy VIIa remains elusive.

Which destruction is due to the Greeks, to the Trojan War? Troy VI seemed to better match the Troy portrayed in *Iliad*. It was more prosperous, more worthy of a King Priam. Those who accept that *Iliad* presents an exaggerated view of the size of the Greek forces also look to the Troy VI destruction. They believe that Greeks, hearing that the walls of Troy had tumbled down due to earthquake, assembled a force and struck quickly in a raid or limited attack.

Those who take Homer's *Iliad* more literally as history favor the second destruction, that of Troy VIIa. There was great damage and that better matches the consequences of an attack by a big Greek force as described in *Iliad*. A date as late as 1150 BC raises difficulties, however. Mycenaean Greece with its palaces and citadels had already begun its steep decline, the descent into the Dark Age. Greeks of that time would have been ill-equipped for a foreign adventure.

If a Trojan War, or minor skirmishes which led to the Trojan War story, were to be dated after about 1200 BC, report of it will not be found in Hittite records. By then, the Hittite empire and its record-keepers had disappeared.

Comparing Evidence

Allowance must be made for two different dating methods, each of which has uncertainties. Historical records for the date of King Muwatalli are reliable. (He fought against the Egyptians in the Battle of Kadesh). While it is not completely certain that it was this king to whom Manapa-Tarhunda wrote, it is supported by high historic probability. Pottery evidence, on the other hand, has only been able to supply a broad range of possible dates for the destruction of Troy VI. Yet the dates of reign of Muwatalli fall neatly within the range of those pottery dates, and that supports the view that it was Troy VI that was attacked by Greek forces.

Other Wars and Other Times

There are other records that seem to reflect Greek activities in western Anatolia. Greeks appear to have had a hand in the war between the Assuwa Confederation and the Hittites.

A letter from the archives tells that Seha River Land committed a wrong against the Hittites, and the Greek king withdrew either his presence or his support from Seha River Land. The date of this activity is not known.

Another Hittite letter, to a vassal king, discusses Walmu. He was a former king of Troy, in exile and living under the protection of the vassal king. The Hittites wanted to re-install Walmu as king in Troy. At the same time, the Hittite king wrote that he wanted to revise the borders of Miletus. Was Walmu deposed by a Greek invasion of Troy? That the Hittites were prepared to revise the borders of Miletus and felt free to do so, suggests a diplomatic rupture with the Greeks.

Then there is a directive to a Hittite vassal king in Syria. Stop Greek ships from offloading merchandise bound for Assyria. That also suggests a breach of relations with Greece.

To summarize, the following have been mentioned: Greek participation in a war in support of Assuwa and against the Hittites; attacks of Attarissiyas, a Greek, on Madduwatta, a Hittite vassal; an attack on Troy per the Manapa-Tarhunda Letter; the above note about Walmu and the borders of Miletus; withdrawal of the Greek king from support of Seha River Land.

The Hittite records which have been mentioned span nearly two centuries. It can be taken as certain that what now remains of the records cannot reflect all of Greek activities in western Anatolia. Many incidents were probably not worth reporting to the Hittite king by vassal kings, and many records may simply have been retained in the archives of the vassals. It is a tragedy of historic knowledge that none of these vassal archives have been found, including that of Troy, for it is certain that those vassal regimes were literate.

Which Is the Trojan War

All of the Greek activities were remembered for at least some time by participants and their descendants. Some memories survived longer than others in various Greek families or Greek communities. As the stories were recalled and retold in a non-literate Dark Age, they lost time tags, and even place tags. However, the attack on Seha River Land and Troy seem to have produced the most important memories, surviving in the works of Homer, Archilochus, Cypria and into the literate age.

Events from the Bronze Age provided a body of lore which was exploited by the poet-singers. It is curious that the language of *Iliad* reveals an Aeolic dialect substratum. Aeolic was the dialect of Lesbos in the Classical period. It is at least possible, perhaps likely, that the Greeks who with Piyama-Radu attacked Lesbos left people there, at Lesbos. Perhaps it was they who first preserved a story of an attack on Seha River Land and Wilusa, that is on Mysia and Troy.

8

ORALITY AND TRADITION

It is possible that the tall of a Trojan War originated in Lesbos and that it was preserved there by those speaking in an early Aeolian dialect. The story may have been maintained in Lesbos until Ionians to the south of them encountered the tale. Alternatively, the story may have crossed the Aegean with back-migrants, to Aeolian-speaking Thessaly. There it may have been maintained, and then have crossed the narrow strait to Euboea. Perhaps Homer encountered it there. Nearby was Aulis, which both *Iliad* and Cypria claim as the assembly point of the Greek host. Nearby also was the place where Hesiod won a prize in a poetry contest. These are among the unsolved problems.

There are scholars who maintain that nothing of the Bronze Age came through to Homer. Indeed, there is a gap of over four hundred years between the end of the Bronze Age and the time of Homer. That is a long time, enough time for any memories of the Bronze Age to be forgotten or distorted. There was no written history, no means by which the thread of memory, once broken, could be restored. And if there was no memory from the Bronze Age in *Iliad*, or in Cypria, then the Trojan War is fiction. In that case, the archaeologists at Hissarlik are not working at Troy but at just another ruin, interesting though that may be, and their work loses some of its luster. Scholars who look for the "historic" Troy would be chasing a dream less substantial than that of Camelot.

If there is nothing of the Bronze Age in *Iliad*, then all of the events and all of the color are taken from Homer's own time or a time not long before. As an example, Homer describes chariot warfare. The combatants rush to the scene of battle, and there they dismount to fight. The chariot is no more than a taxi. Some scholars believe that Homer did not know that warriors in the Bronze Age fought with spear and bow from a charging chariot. In fact, Homer may have been right. Illustrations of the battle of Kadesh at the temple at Medinet Habu in Egypt show Bronze Age Hittites in combat. Their chariots were manned by a crew of three. This should be understood as a driver, a chariot combatant, and a drop-off combatant, rushed to the place of battle. By no means was all terrain suitable for charging chariots. What should be done with idle chariots? The ability to use chariots to rapidly move combatants to the place of need, where they would dismount, may be taken for granted (see Appendix G).

Other scholars are troubled that Homer mentions iron. How can there be iron if Homer is reporting of the Bronze Age? In fact, iron was known and used in the Bronze Age, though very sparingly, since the technology of iron manufacture was not widely understood. Reflecting this scarcity, Homer reports that iron was set out as a prize—a rare material— at the funeral games for Patroclus. Such a report would be fully consistent with the high value of iron in the Late Bronze Age. Homer also says that iron could be given to a farmer to make a plow shear, thus suggesting a rather lower value of iron. That would be consistent with the value of iron in Homer's time. The treatment of iron in *Iliad* illustrates what is nearly certain, that *Iliad* mixes knowledge from different time periods.

Does *Iliad* contain any memory of the Bronze Age? Possibly. There are the boar's tusk helmet, the body shield, and more. That helmet is described in *Iliad*. Sections of boars tusk were sewn to a leather cap that was worn to protect the head. Such a helmet is shown on the head of a small ivory figure found at Mycenae, and on Mycenaean frescos, and is authentic to the Bronze Age. It was not in use after the Bronze Age, so far as is known. *Iliad also* mentions the body shield which, as the name suggests, was about the length of the body. Such shields are illustrated in Mycenaean frescos and, again, were not used, so far as is known, after the Bronze Age. More examples of possible material survivals from the Bronze Age in *Iliad* might be mentioned.

These are not certain proofs, however, of a memory from the Bronze Age. Material things such as the helmet or shield may have survived well into the Dark Age or later, as heirlooms, or more likely as illustrations in Mycenaean ruins and tombs. These might have thus been known to people of Homer's time, and thus may not be genuine memories preserved over the generations by the poet-singers since the Bronze Age.

There were, however, non-material survivals from the Bronze Age. The language of Homer's time is a descendant of the Greek language of the Bronze Age as known from the Linear B tablets. Vases have been excavated in various parts of Greece representing various time periods. These bridge the gap between the Bronze Age and the Classical period. On some of these vases, there are Bronze Age decorative elements, thus showing continuity of certain design ideas from that time. Martin Nilsson in his book about Greek mythology (see Readings) shows that Greek myths from the Bronze Age survived thru the Dark Age even to the Classical period when they were used by playwrights and storytellers.

Many of the Greek gods known from Linear B tablets of the Bronze Age were still revered in the time of Homer, and beyond.

These include Zeus, Hera, Poseidon, Athena. Interesting, and perhaps telling, Apollo does not appear among the gods mentioned in these tablets. In the Bronze Age, Apollo was not a Greek god but a Trojan god. Homer apparently knew that, knew of the Greek gods of the Bronze Age, and seemingly knew that Apollo was not one of them.[8.1]

Thus the Dark Age was not an impenetrable barrier. That much is evident. It is safe, therefore, to assume that there came to Homer stories from the Bronze Age, and that would include stories dealing with events in western Anatolia, as described in the previous chapter. However, with telling and retelling, over generations, these stories changed in significant ways. It is usually held that any story can survive more or less intact over about three generations. The grandfather fought in the battle. As he tells the tale to his sons and grandsons, he may exaggerate his role and his heroism to some extent, but he is still alive to correct the son or grandson about essential features of the story. After that time, the story drifts, loses its moorings, and there is no way to correct the drift away from the historic truth. Tales coming from the Bronze Age were modified bit by bit over the years, by replacement of elements of the story, by exaggeration, and by fusion with other memories.

Multiple Stories

It is a mistake when thinking of ancient Greece to always think in terms of Athens. Most Greeks lived in the countryside. In their villages and towns, tales were told, at mother's knee, at the fireside, in places where men gathered. A degree of isolation prevailed, yet tales moved about, place to place. Many were casually told tales, but people looked to the serious storyteller, the poet-singer, for information and entertainment. Unlike the casual storyteller, the poet-singer could provide connected plot and colorful description, and a beautiful poetic language, and his charismatic skill held the listeners. Such was the craft that Homer practiced.

The way in which stories moved among villages, and among poet-singers, the effect of decades and centuries of telling and retelling, resulted in the splitting of tales into various versions—essentially the same story told differently. The singer, including Homer, had many stories available to him, and in some cases several versions.

Multiple stories are evident in *Odyssey*. Few believe that the composer of *Odyssey* invented those tales out of nothing, tales of one-eyed monsters, seductive witches, and more. Surely, he inherited those yarns and artfully combined or reshaped them according to his need. Surely his audience enjoyed hearing those tales again, now retold by a master artist. In *Iliad*, as examples, stories of Bellerophon and the fire-breathing monster[6.1] and of Meleager and the hunt for the monster boar, probably were separate stories before they were brought together by Homer, or his predecessors.

In *Iliad* and Cypria, there are traces of multiple versions of the same story. These traces are evident in the form of doublets. Two different versions of the attack on Troy have already been mentioned. There is also a story of an attack on Troy well before that of the Greeks under Agamemnon. This earlier attack was led by Heracles. In effect, there are three versions of a Greek attack on Troy. There are doublets and triplets of certain names in *Iliad*. Two different names of the city, Ilios and Troy, are an example, see Appendix H. While each such might perhaps be explained away by a rationalization, or a harmonization, the most likely explanation is that Homer knew multiple versions of the tale of Troy and blended them together.[8.2]

The Unhistorical Poet

Poet-singers, attempting to tell of events of a remote past, do not deal with these events as a historian would. Even those recent poet-singers of Bosnia, living in an age of literacy, did not think in historical terms. They did not have the training. They could not check facts. They did not delve into history books dealing with the time of which they sang, even if such books existed. They did not understand the concept that we call "history." Only the story mattered, and so it was with Homer. He would attempt, so far as he could, so far as his limited knowledge would allow, to position his tale in a correct ancient environment. Beyond that, his skill was used to tell a tale, to tell of glorious deeds and of heroism, and of tragedy. These things carried lessons for his time, and justified his work. The possible existence in his time of limited literacy would make no difference.

Once the original tale is loosed from its moorings in the remote past, once it is taken up by poet-singers over the generations, with none knowing about history, the story would take on a strange coloration. This can be learned by an examination of various stories of a later age that developed under similar conditions of illiteracy or semi-literacy. Think of *Iliad* when you read next.

Atlakvida and Nibelunglied

These are stories from the Middle Ages in Europe. Atlakvida from the Poetic Eddas of Iceland was put into writing about AD 1270. It tells that Atli, king of the Huns, covets the gold of King Gunnarr of Burgundy. Atli invites Gunnarr to a feast seeking to wheedle out of him the location of the gold. In the course of events, Atli kills Gunnarr. Atli's wife, who happens to be the sister of Gunnarr, kills Atli in revenge.

Nibelunglied is the German version of that tale, in writing about AD 1200. The plot is too complicated to tell here. Listen to Wagner's opera. But there is an Etzel, king of the Huns, Gunther king of Burgundy, and Brunhilde. A conflict occurs between the Huns and Burgundians and Etzel is killed, as are the Burgundians. The conflict was stirred up by Etzel's wife, according to this version.

The historic basis of both stories is the invasion of the Huns and their slaughter of the Burgundians in AD 437. Atli in the Icelandic version and Etzel in the German tale are Attila. He died at the hands of a woman in AD 454. There was a Gundaharius upon whom Gunnarr and Gunther were based. There was an historical Brunechildis who lived more than a century after those events.

The two stories differ from one another in detail, so that one or both have diverged from actual historic events. However, in these stories, an actual historic conflict or battle is remembered, of the Huns and Burgundians, and the main participants are correctly recalled. But one, Brunhilde, is of another time, yet has been brought into the story.

The Tale of Kosovo

Among the Christian Bosnians, oral poetry existed into recent times though not as well maintained as among Muslim Bosnians. Christian Bosnian oral tradition told of the Battle of Kosovo in which Christian Serbs fought Muslim Turkish forces. The battle took place in AD 1389. Here, Marko Kraljević, who died in 1394, is in the Kosovo story. But so is Vuk Branković, who died in 1486, more than 90 years later. Also, the brothers Mrnjavćević are said to have fought in the battle of Kosovo. But they actually died 18 years earlier, in the battle of Marica.

Again, an historic battle is remembered, and a hero of that battle. But heroes from a later and an earlier battle have been brought into the story.

A few generations after the Battle of Kosovo, a Turkish historian collected tales from Muslim peasants in the Balkans, tales preserved orally. They tell that at Kosovo, the Christian Serb army consisted of 500,000 infantry commanded by 500 princes supported by 300,000 knights on white horses. There are no reliable records of the actual size of the Christian Serb force, but the Turkish force was reported to be not more than 9,000. The Christian force was probably no larger.

The Song of Roland

The Song of Roland was composed in about AD 1100 and was popular in the time of the crusades. The historical event upon which it was based occurred in AD 778. There a gap of about 300 years during which the tale appears to have survived in part by oral transmission. The Song tells of the withdrawal of Charlemagne's army from Spain. Roland is in charge of the rear guard of the retreating army. As that army passes through the Pyrenees, a Muslim army with some forces under the leadership of the Emir of far-off Babylon overwhelm the rear guard. Roland dies heroically. The Muslim army is described as vast in number, 400,000 men, and gain advantage through treachery.

The story is based on the return of Charlemagne from Spain. Records confirm that there was a Roland who was a baron under Charlemagne. Charlemagne was in Spain at the invitation of his Muslim friend, an Emir in Saragossa. In his passage through the Pyrenees, the rear guard was attacked by some Basques in response to pillaging by the retreating army. There was no treachery, no vast Muslim army, and probably no Muslims at all. In the Song of Roland, there are a number of other barons. Some of these barons were not historic contemporaries of Roland, but lived up to a century later.

Memories of Ibrahim Pasha

During the Ottoman Empire, a war lord named Ibrahim Pasha moved his army through Cilicia in Turkey. He cleared a road for his big guns to pass and little more. A few generations later, a British traveler noted that the local population identified every ancient building, every stone bridge, as the work of Ibrahim Pasha. This illustrates how quickly the legend of a hero may develop.

Patterns

The following pattern is evident. Though these stories contain much that is fictional, in Atlakvida, Nibelunglied, the Song of Roland, and the story of Kosovo, actual historic battles were remembered. Several persons central to the historic event were also remembered. However, other people from different periods were brought into the story. Further, in the Kosovo story, two different battles fought at different times were combined, so that it is evident that two stories were merged. In both Roland and Kosovo, the number of combatants was greatly exaggerated.

From these examples, the following can be believed about *Iliad*. The story is likely based on an actual ancient conflict. However, it need not have been a full scale war. But it was at least a battle or a raid sufficient to create reports of kleos, that is, deeds of renown. The size of the opposing forces in *Iliad* has been greatly inflated. The size of the Greek force can be determined from the count of ships given in *Iliad*. That provides an estimate of as many as 60,000 men, or more, which is unbelievable.

One or more leading figures in *Iliad* are probably authentic to the time, place, and conflict. Agamemnon probably falls into this category. Many other participants derive from some other time or place. Ajax came from a different time because of his full body shield. Likewise, Odysseus and Idomeneus, and many others, were probably drawn into the story by the magnetic power of the growing epic.

More than one historical conflict may have been merged into the tale of Troy. Such events could have occurred in distant places. In the Bronze Age, Greek ships sailed to the coast of Syria in trade. The incident, mentioned in the previous chapter, in which the Hittite king ordered his vassal in Syria to prevent offloading from Greek ships testifies to that. Ugarit was a great city on the Syrian coast. In about 1190 BC—good Egyptian correlations exist for this date—Ugarit was attacked from the sea and sent up in flames. Some belief that this was the work of the Peoples of the Sea and that Greeks were among them. News of this would have been known in every Greek port in that same sailing season. This would have been a wonderful addition to the lore of poet-singers, a great city by the sea attacked and set ablaze, and might have become part of the story of Troy (see Appendix I).

Homer took what he had inherited from the past and these probably formed a kaleidoscope of stories. He gave thought to a great work, how these past stories might be used. How an audience might be held. And what would be the audience for such a great work?

9

VENUE

What was a full day's work for a poet-singer? The work of Milman Parry and Alfred Lord in the Balkans in the 1930s provided a wonderful laboratory in which to explore that question. Lord noted that a day's performance by a Bosnian poet-singer amounted to the delivery of about 1,000 verse lines after which the performer was exhausted. One singer, Avdo Mededović of marvelous endurance, delivered an epic of the length of *Odyssey*. It took over three weeks. He worked for several days in the first and third weeks. In the second week he stopped because he needed to rest. That amounted to about 1,600 verse lines a day in the two working weeks.

Turning back to the Greeks, Hesiod's *Theogony* is about 1,000 verse lines. It was this work that Hesiod may have performed at the funeral games of Amphidamas in Euboea and won a prize. A nice day's work. The limit of what should be asked of a poet-singer.

Parry describes the effort required of a Bosnian poet-singer-

> ... a voice as strong as possible singing as high a pitch as possible, a clear cut and forceful delivery of the words, and a vigorous accompaniment upon the instrument. It takes the full strength of a man to sing this way. The movement of the body in playing the instrument, the labor of the lungs for the breath needed for the volume of song, the strain on the muscles of the throat and mouth that go to forming the words, make the singing a toil,

and a good singer after a half hour of his song is drenched in sweat ...

In addition to the physical strain, Parry might have mentioned the mental strain.

Iliad is about 15,000 verses long, and *Odyssey* is only slightly shorter. This is not of a length typical of a poet-singer, but much more. If anything, the Greek would be harder to deliver than that in the Bosnian language of Avdo Mededovic' for the Greek meter is more demanding. The physical demands of performing a work of the length of *Iliad* raise a question. Did Homer ever deliver *Iliad* in a live performance? Did he intend to?

Paying the Poet

A basket of food, a drink, and later a choice cut of meat were set before Demodocus, we learn from *Odyssey*, but these were only to sustain him during his performance. Beyond the pleasure that the poet-singer took in his craft, beyond the esteem in which he was held by his audience because of his skill, the performer needed some other recompense to support him over the longer term. Hesiod was a farmer and sheep keeper, and that provided for his needs, but not every performer could count on such resource.

In the case of the Bosnian poet-singer Avdo Mededovic,' not only did he have a trade but a substantial purse was gathered for him as thanks and reward for a longer performance. As for Homer, his economic circumstances are unknown to us. Considering the length of *Iliad*, a basket of food and a slab of meat would, of course, be out of the question. There must have been in Greece, particularly as it emerged from the darkness of centuries, some intermediate vehicle of economic compensation, something we would call money.

Hesiod, who lived at a time and a place not far distant from Homer hints at this when he tells of outfitting a ship for trade in order to produce a profit. In the distant past, in the Bronze Age, silver was the intermediate vehicle, and archaeologists have found scales used to measure out silver. Silver may have been available for that purpose in Homer's time from the silver mines of Attica just across the Aegean. Homer lived not in some Elysian Field but in the real world, and when the possible venues for performance of *Iliad* are considered, the ability to pay the poet must be considered.

Venue

The tavern, the warm smithy's hovel where men gathered in winter as Hesiod said in order to keep warm, the occasional village or market fair and other such small gatherings would not be appropriate venues for a work of the length and scope of *Iliad*. Nor could they produce much reward. Competitions were held at funerals but, by their nature, they were too short. A wedding would have been a poor venue. They are notoriously boisterous. In *Odyssey*, Homer describes a wedding feast given in Sparta by Helen and Menelaus. A poet-singer had barely started when he was upstaged by acrobats. Hardly the required setting for a large work. A great political assembly, a hypothetical pan-Ionic league for example, would have been suitable, but there is no evidence for such a gathering in the time of Homer, whenever that may have been. One can think of some rich household in Ionia willing to entertain guests over many days. Such might be suitable for a performance of *Iliad* and might produce a suitable purse. But this situation is artificial as there is no evidence at all to support it.

That there was a venue for performance of *Iliad* is obvious, but no sure knowledge of it remains. It becomes a matter of speculation, of searching for a model situation. The clearest model is the gathering on the island of Delos.

There was a shrine of the god Apollo on Delos. Every four years, before the Classical period, there was a gathering in honor of the god. The gathering must have had somewhat of the spirit of a holiday vacation. In the surviving Hymn to Apollo, which was probably performed there, it is said that well-off Ionians came to the event together with their wives and children. As transportation was not easy, it is likely that they came to stay for at least a number of days, perhaps longer. As part of the activity, poetical works were performed.

In the United States in the late 1800s and early 1900s, there was a religious revival that featured "camp meetings." Here, people gathered for many days or weeks to hear sermons, socialize, and recreate as at Ocean Grove, New Jersey. The ancient gathering on Delos must have been similar.

With the amount of time available to the poet singer, a long work could be performed. People had nowhere else to go and little else to do. Here a good purse might be gathered, and the audience would appreciate a skillful performance. It isn't known if a gathering at Delos existed in Homer's time, but it should be recalled that the story of *Iliad* is launched with the supernatural attack on the Greek camp by Apollo. The subject matter of *Iliad* would have been suitable for the shrine of Apollo at Delos. If not this then some other convocation, perhaps of the nature of an early Ionian political gathering, might also have provided suitable conditions.

Oral Presentation

The available evidence is against the performance of any long work by a single poet-singer, including Homer. The athletic demands of performance, the extraordinary length of *Iliad* or *Odyssey*, the difficulty of identifying a venue in which the works could be performed with attention by an audience, seem to lead to a conclusion.

These works by Homer were never performed by him. That is, they were never performed on an oral basis in which the work was entirely created in performance, before an audience. Even before the Classical period, in Athens, there was a festival, the Panathenaic festival, dedicated to the goddess Athena. It is said that there the works of Homer were performed by rhapsodists. Rhapsodists performed not by creation in performance as did poet-singers, but by reading from a text. It is further said that, for this purpose, the Homeric text was divided up and assigned to different rhapsodists in relay. Nothing could more clearly say that, so far as the ancient Athenians believed, the work of Homer could not be performed end to end by one man on an oral basis.

Iliad into Writing

Since *Iliad* shows ample evidence of oral composition, it is natural to assume that Homer lived in a time before writing came to Greece. Or, if writing in some early form existed, Homer did not avail of it. On that assumption, how is it that today we have a written text? A simple explanation might be that *Iliad* was transmitted by oral means from Homer's time into the future, perhaps over several generations, to such time that writing was common in Greece and such a large work could have been easily committed for the first time to writing.

The problems with this are manifold. The existence of an oral performance of *Iliad* by Homer seems unlikely, but let us suppose such a performance. This performance must have been heard by a younger poet-singer, who would be the first link in a chain of oral transmission, poet-singer to poet-singer over the generations. He heard and he learned, the complete *Iliad*, about 15,700 verse lines, containing mention of about 1.000 different people and places.

To have preserved *Iliad* this way would have required of him a memorization on a vast scale for which there is hardly any precedent. It is true that in India the Rig-Vida, a work many times the length of *Iliad*, was preserved, word for word it is believed, by memory over the generations. There was a strong religious and liturgical motive for preservation of the Rig-Vida, and it is likely that such memorization by a novice performer began in youth and extended over much of a lifetime. *Iliad* had no such religious imperative, and no facility for teaching over a lifetime.[91]

The presumed motivation of the younger poet-singer would only have been that he would perform *Iliad* and gain acclaim, and that would also be the motive of his successors in turn, down the generations.

But if it was *Iliad* that was preserved that way, if it was *Iliad* that was performed, this means that the work was learned down to the very words that Homer used. However, such word for word learning is not the way a poet-singer worked. He worked by re-creation, mostly in his own words, a fresh performance every time. That this is so is shown by evidence from Bosnia and many places where there are oral performers.

Iliad is noted for near-perfection of scene, characterization, and especially language. If transmitted by generations of poet-singers, working according to their traditional ways, it could not help but loose that perfection, because those transmitters had not Homer's creative genius. Sir Walter Scott was a collector of Scotch ballads, ballads transmitted largely orally. Scott noted that with each oral repetition of a work, it became more flat, more insipid.

If, on the other hand, the final performance in this chain of transmission leading to writing was given by another poet-singer of genius, then it was the words of this later poet-singer that now constitutes the written *Iliad* that we have. Then, all of the merits of *Iliad* noted over all ages would be due to him. That situation comes close to the joke told by Homer teachers. "*Iliad* was not composed by Homer, but by another man of the same name."

It seems that there is no escaping this conclusion. *Iliad* could not have been transmitted by oral means, and that is so whether the term "oral" represents singer's recreation or even pure memorization. Thus, *Iliad* must have been committed to writing in the time of Homer, and inescapably with the participation of Homer.

That conclusion may seem strange, because it had been thought that Homer lived in an illiterate age. Further, based on experience gained in Bosnia, Parry and Lord concluded that literacy suppresses or drives out the oral performance art. Yet both accept that Homer participated in the writing of *Iliad*.[9.2] Studies of oral performance in parts of the world other that Bosnia show, however, that writing and oral performance may not be entirely incompatible.

Richard Janko studied the poetic language used by Homer and Hesiod. The works of both are in the same Ionic poet's language. But language changes over time and Janko applied the science of glottochronology to their surviving works. He was able to establish a relative dating for *Iliad*, *Odyssey*, and Hesiod's *Theogony*, that is, a relative date of their writing. This shows that *Iliad* was composed before *Odyssey*, as has long been suspected, and *Theogony* later than both.

Theogony is set at about 70 years after *Iliad*. Thus, about 70 years after *Iliad*, in the face of writing, Hesiod was still able to compose in the language, the vocabulary and diction, of oral poetry. That would confirm that even during a period in which writing was spreading, the poetic language and its use by poet-singers was fully preserved. A long overlap of oral composition and writing is indicated.

Dictation

As noted earlier, the adaptation of the Phoenician alphabet by the Greeks may have been driven by the need to put the work of the poet-singers into writing. It must be assumed that *Iliad* was planned from the beginning to be written. Perhaps the easiest possibility is that Homer dictated *Iliad* to a man skilled in writing, a scribe. Parry carried out an experiment in which a Bosnian poet-singer dictated a work to a scribe. The trial was said to be successful. Of course, anything can be dictated, and Parry did not report on the quality of the dictated work.

The problems involved in dictation in the time of Homer would have been formidable. There are many skills involved in writing now taken for granted which may not have existed in Ionia of Homer's time. Direction of the written line, stance of the characters, spelling, all may have still been in flux. Ability to make revisions, do deletes, spelling changes, all would still have been in the future. Nor could the scribe have had the skill of a modern stenographer. His writing must have been slow and laborious. Setting up the parchments, if that is what was used, sharpening the pen, blotting, refreshing the ink, all are annoying interruptions to the work.

Parry reported that poet-singers must be rapid in order to develop their metric verses. Could Homer have worked with the painful slowness required of dictation? One can imagine the problem. *"Now when the men of both sides were set in order by their leaders ..."* Homer says. "Did you get that down? No? Must I repeat it? Now where was I?" Now Homer needs a break. Soon the scribe needs a break.

A project such as described involving poet, scribe, masses of parchment, an extensive amount of time and labor may have involved economic stress, and perhaps a "patron" was involved. That intriguing possibility is not explored further here.

Homer as a Writer

The alternative is that Homer wrote *Iliad*, without help. This possibility does not alleviate all problems of dictation, but eases some of them. It is true that, in the Hymn to Apollo, there is an allusion to the blind singer from Chios and that is taken to refer to Homer. Here, a belief may have arisen that Homer was blind because Demodocus of *Odyssey* was blind. Suppose that he was not blind. The similes for which *Iliad* is famous are largely visual. The Bosnian poet-singer, Avdo Mededovic,' said that first he would visualize an action, then he put the vision to words. Such may have been Homer's way also.

It is by no means impossible that Homer could have been both a poetic composer and a writer. Present-day musicians compose, and they easily set down their work in the notes of musical writing. Why should not a dual skill have been possible for Homer? We can imagine that Homer, as a youth, followed the usual progression: learning the poet-singer craft from a master, then performing on his own perhaps 1,000 or so verse lines, gradual perfecting his skill. At the same time, writing was "in the air," talked about by many. There probably were experiments already undertaken before Homer to put short poems into writing. As a young man, Homer may have become fascinated by this new technology. He may have been an "early adapter." It would not have been hard for a person of a mind inclined to words. One sound, one symbol, and the symbols are easily drawn.

He may have thought about *Iliad* for years. Writing might allow the composition of a great work, greater by far than could be done on the basis of a thousand or so lines of poetry. As a poet-singer, many stories were known to him relating to a Trojan War, and others which could be reshaped and brought into the story.

Now, without a scribe, Homer's thoughts need not be interrupted. Before setting words in writing, he could turn over in his mind lines of verse, and in his mind rapidly change phrasing, and consider alternatives. This is not even possible to do in oral performance and may explain the perfection of Homer's composition. This could not be easily done while dictating to a scribe, and this seems to be the most likely course.

It thus seems probable that Homer not only composed but wrote *Iliad*. It is likely that Homer was a transitional poet-singer in the sense noted in Chapter 2. One purpose suggests itself for the composition of this great work. And that purpose will answer many questions.

Homeridae

If *Iliad* could not be performed by Homer in the manner that earlier, shorter, works were performed, before an audience, then he might have intended from the beginning to divide the work among several performers. This is exactly how the works of Homer were performed by the rhapsodists in Athens centuries later. This would require a written text so that sections might be assigned to various performers. One thinks of the Homeridae.

The term means sons of Homer, or descendants of Homer, or at least followers of Homer. The Classical period poet Pindar referred to them. They lived before his time, on Chios. Their task was to perform and thus preserve the works of Homer. In those times, as in all ages, sons followed their father's trade or craft and it is possible that the first generation of Homeridae were Homer's sons. In that view, the purpose of the great composition was to provide an occupation and an income for his sons.

It is they who must have been the rhapsodists who first performed *Iliad*. It is to them, according to this view, that we owe the earlier preservation and dissemination of *Iliad* and *Odyssey*.

10

WRITING AND TRANSMISSION

Iliad has survived and come down to us over a span of 2700 or more years. It would be enlightening and rewarding if the details of how this was accomplished were known. There is little knowledge of this, particularly for the years before the Classical period. There are a few facts, however, upon which some speculation can be based and it is necessary to depend on likelihoods and probabilities.

Homer may have lived and worked a few years before 700 BC. Even before his time, there must have been experiments in putting poetry into writing. Then, a written *Iliad* was produced by Homer, or with his collaboration. It must have burst upon the Greek world as a surprise, if the term "burst" can be used to characterize communications in those early times. A written *Iliad*, because of its length, and the publicity arising from a performance at Delos or a Delos-like venue, would have a profound effect, and hastened the spread of writing.

Other works of which we have some knowledge were composed at about that time, or perhaps slightly later. These include the Hymn to Apollo and certain other hymns, and works of Hesiod. Some of these may have been composed in writing. Yet, as with *Iliad*, they reflect the poet-singer's diction. Some works of the Homeric Cycle may be of this period, but nothing is known of their origin or survival.

Looking for Homer

As writing spread, it began to be so respected that non-literate poet-singers could no longer find employment in literate parts of Greek world, and their craft retreated to the rural backlands. With writing, new fields of endeavor opened, that of historian for example, for before that time the poet-singer was the only "historian." By whom else could lore of the past have been preserved and transmitted but by poet-singers? By about 650 BC, with the advance of writing, new forms of poetry appeared, that of Archilocus and Semonides, for example.

Through all of these changes, a written text of *Iliad* was maintained.

By the beginning of the Classical period, writing had existed for centuries in the Greek world. Is it possible that there was only one written copy of *Iliad* over that large span of time? That seems very unlikely. The corporation of Homeric performers known as the Homeridae may have ensured the existence of only one copy of *Iliad* as beneficial to them—a monopoly— and maintained that for a time, but such corporations fly apart. There would be a contrary interest in multiple copies before long.

Socrates said that Hipparchus (who died in 514 BC) did a wonderful thing by bringing the works of Homer to his country, by which presumably he meant Athens, and compelling a reading by a team of rhapsodes in relay as noted earlier. That certainly would have required a written text to be partitioned among the rhapsodes. It is unreasonable to believe that, by the time of the Athenian undertaking, they held in their hands the one and only copy of Homer's work.

In about 500 BC, the Persians invaded Ionia and established a puppet regime in Chios, home of the Homeridae. The Persian invasion of Ionia would have induced a concern for the survival and preservation of Athenian-Ionian culture. What more important monument of that culture than *Iliad* and *Odyssey*? What better way to preserve them than through ensuring that there were copies?

Herodotus, Thucydides, Plato and Aristotle, refer to the works of Homer. These were literate men who wrote copiously, and it seems unlikely that they would not have a written *Iliad* text before them, that they would simply depend on memory from a rhapsode performance. It can be taken as certain that multiple copies of *Iliad* existed during the early years of the Classical period, and probably earlier, perhaps much earlier.

Search for the Correct *Iliad*

Since the Classical period, many in the Greek world looked to *Iliad* as a guide to morals and to models of behavior. It is a nice story that Alexander (356 BC–323 BC), a pupil of Aristotle, carried a copy of *Iliad* around in a silver box. It is believable. According to *Iliad*, Achilles was the son of a goddess. Alexander believed that he too was descended from a god and probably received what he considered to be confirmation of that from the priests of Ammon in Egypt. Alexander was, in his own eyes, the new Achilles and indeed he imitated Achilles' pathological carnage.

After the conquest of Egypt by Alexander, Greek rule there was established under Greek general Ptolemy. His descendants ruled in Egypt for several centuries. Greek colonists came and settled, not only in the "new" city of Alexandria, but in towns along the Nile. It is likely that among the first wave were retired soldiers who were settled by the Ptolemies, just as later the Romans settled retired soldiers in Syria and Anatolia. The Greeks who came had literate people among them. That is known since fragments of a variety of Greek writings have been found in the ruins of some of these towns. Some of these fragments are from ancient trash dumps, tombs, and even mummy wrappings, which indicates that these towns had both Greek and Egyptian residents. Among the text fragments were parts of *Iliad* and *Odyssey*.

Imagine the shock to some modern scholars when it was found that poetic lines of *Iliad* or *Odyssey* in these fragments differed from our present-day versions of these works. A fragment of *Iliad* found in Hibah in upper Egypt, from the period of the Ptolemies, contained several dozen lines of verse not found in the present text. Also, many "correct" lines of verse were missing. An *Iliad* fragment from a period after the Ptolemies likewise showed differences from our present text. Again, new lines had been inserted. Old lines were dropped. Most of the added lines, but not all, were transposed from other parts of *Iliad*. This instability in the text had an even earlier history. Plato (428 BC–348 BC) quoted lines from *Iliad* somewhat different from those in our present text.

These findings raise a question. Is our present-day *Iliad* the correct version? Or, did a correct version exist only in some distant past? That question has set scholars on a search for the "vulgate." The definition of such vulgate is somewhat uncertain, but the vulgate *Iliad* would be the "authorized," or "correct" or "Homeric" version.

Under the Ptolemies, the Library of Alexandria in Egypt was established. To this library were gathered texts on many subjects from all over the Greek-speaking world and from other regions that Alexander had conquered. It is estimated that over 40,000 texts were kept there. Ptolemy II (283 BC–246 BC) brought scholars from Judah to Alexandria to produce a translation into Greek of the Hebrew Bible, probably intended for the library. That translation survives in the Septuagint text.

The Library of Alexandria was more than a book repository. It was also an outstanding institution for scholarly study. There were scholars who studied the Homeric texts, and presumably they had copies from various sources available to them. One of these scholars, Zenodotus (325 BC–260 BC), saw trouble in the texts of *Iliad* open before him. He was certain that *Iliad* had been corrupted. *Iliad* was to him a beautiful flower garden now infested with weeds. It needed weeding, and he went about that vigorously. He indicated by margin notes where he found missing lines and where he found spurious or intruded lines. His work was furthered by a successor, Aristarchus (220 BC–143 BC). How these men recognized errors in *Iliad* is not certain, but comparison among texts was obviously involved. So was taste, and they marking off vulgarities, as it seemed to them, as unworthy of Homer. That also played a role in their decisions. It seems clear that they had no "vulgate," no authoritative text before them as a standard of comparison since, if such had existed, there would have been no need of their work.

It is likely that there were copies of *Iliad* in the Classical period and certainly so in the time of the Ptolemies. In all of that time, who, or what institution, had any authority or power to maintain or enforce a standard text? There were no copyrights, no publishers, no rulers with that power or with such concerns. It is said that the Athenian ruler Peisistratus, who lived at the threshold of the Classical period, oversaw the creation of a standard text but, if that even occurred, the effort at standardization was unsuccessful, ephemeral. What effect would his rules have had in Sparta, or in Corinth?

What of the Homeridae? If ever they were concerned with textual purity, that concern apparently was gone by the time of Plato. Plato describes a conversation between Socrates and a rhapsode named

Ion. Ion tells Socrates that he has made some beautiful changes to Homer and would be glad to recite those. Maybe some other time, says Socrates. Ion says that his changes are so beautiful that the Homeridae should give him a gold crown. It appears from this that the Homeridae were open to changes so long as they were improvements. Homeridae of the time of Socrates were not enforcers of purity, and neither was any other person or group.

Homer himself would not have understood the concept of a vulgate. To poet-singers such as Homer there was no such thing as a standard or correct version. If Homer performed part of *Iliad* before an audience, and performed the same part again at some other time, they might be different from one another.

After the Greek Period

The Romans ruled much of the territory conquered by Alexander and were strongly influenced by Greek culture. Fragments of *Iliad* manuscript have been found representing both early and late periods of Roman rule. These fragments, some fairly long, also show variation in content. Apparently, the "corrections" made by Zenodotus and Aristarchus of the Library of Alexandria years earlier had at best only limited influence. Their corrections could not reach all places in the Roman world where copies of *Iliad* were being made and, in any case, carried little persuasive and no enforcing power.

In Byzantium, ancient Greek learning was preserved at a late date. Around AD 950 a remarkable document, now known as Venetus A, was produced there. It contains 327 pages, and in those pages are scholarly discussions of issues relating to Homeric works, summaries of most of the stories of the Trojan Cycle sometimes attributed to Homer, and notes on the editorial work of Aristarchus.

Most important, it contains the earliest now existing complete copy of *Iliad*.

This valuable document left Byzantium for Italy under unclear circumstances. Possibly the disruptions of the Crusades played a role. Or perhaps it was the migration of Greek scholars from Byzantium to Italy in the 1400s. At sometime in the 1400s, it came into the hands of Cardinal Bessarion, a collector of Greek manuscripts. He gave his collection, including this document, to the library of the Republic of Venice from which came the name of the document. There it lay, forgotten. In time, it was rediscovered by scholars and translations were made. Present-day translations of *Iliad* into English ultimately derive from this Greek text.

It may be thought that the *Iliad* text lived through too much time to reflect the original work of Homer. However, it appears that the changes to the text of *Iliad* were small in total and were not random but concentrated in a few less significant areas. If there had been large changes or additions to *Iliad* after the time of Homer, they would have been evident in the language which would reflect the dialect of a later date.

It is likely, and one hopes that it is so, that the great majority of the lines of the present-day *Iliad* are true to Homer.

AFTERWORD

The title of this book is *Looking For Homer-Finding the Trojan War*.

As for "Finding the Trojan War," the source of the Trojan War story has been traced with reasonable probability in these pages. It lies in a Bronze Age conflict at Wilusa-Troy. The story expanded over time, in the retelling, and by gathering to it other tales of heroes and heroic deeds.

However, "Looking For Homer" has not yielded as much as one would like. Homer remains elusive.

In the year 1948, a movie titled *Treasure of the Sierra* Madre was released, based on a 1927 book of the same title. The author was given as B. Traven. But the name B. Traven was a pseudonym. There was a great effort to find out who this man was. He evaded all efforts to find him, to identify him. He was as unknown as Homer. He was finally tracked down and pressed for his life story. He is reported to have answered only-

The creative person should have no other biography but his works.

Concerning Homer, that is all that can be said and that will need to satisfy us.

NOTES

1.1

For several reasons, dates given for Ages or periods are approximate. There are different assumptions concerning the criteria that denote an Age or period change; the dates are not by their nature very narrowly defined or precise; and the facts are, in any case, not fully known. Thus, there is no agreement among scholars concerning precise dates.

"Recovery period" is used here in place of the commonly used "Archaic period." The term Archaic period derives from a time when earlier archaeologists, working in Greece, found artifacts of that period that seemed backward compared to those of the Classical period. This term is unfortunately negative in implication, and fails to suggest the social and economic changes that took place between the Dark Age and the Classical period.

Certain paragraphs in this Introduction are paraphrased from the author's book *Collapse of the Bronze Age*. See Readings.

1.2

In Kargamish in Syria, a relative of the Hittite king ruled as a viceroy over a small group of nearby city-states. Likely he was served by some functionaries from Hittite Anatolia. This group, and others drawn into the leadership from the local population, thought of themselves as "Hittite." After the collapse of Hittite central power in Anatolia, they preserved this identification as it conferred some elevated standing and legitimacy of rule. That identity was carried forward for generations, and the Assyrians continued to refer to the region of northern Syria as Hittite. The mention of Hittites in the Bible, at a time centuries after the disappearance of Hittite rule in Anatolia, with little doubt refers to these people living close to and in some case in biblical lands.

2.1

This translation from the Greek of Homer by J. H. Dart was an attempt to duplicate, so far as possible, the Homeric hexameter in English. Many readers will find modern translations such as those by Lattimore or Fagles, though not in hexameter, easier to read. See Readings.

2.2

There were two poets—Semonides and Simonides—living almost a century apart with similar and perhaps identical names, sometimes spelled the same way. As their work survives only in incomplete fragments, they are sometimes confused with one another. Semonides of Amorgos is dated about 650 BC, and Simonides of Kea about 470 BC. The conclusion reached about Homer does not change much if the quote is from the earlier or later poet. Dialect is the key. Since the Ionic dialect many have been spoken also in Euboea, the possible territory in which Homer worked might broaden somewhat.

2.3

Said to have been found in the early 1800s on the island of Paros off the Anatolian coast, the Parian Marble in two pieces is inscribed with an ancient Greek chronicle. In the chronicle, dates for what the composer considered to be significant historical events are given, starting in 299 BC, and from that date going backward to a time earlier than 1500 BC. Dates were not given, as here, in terms of BC, but in terms of years before the date at which the chronicle starts. Who the composer was, and the basis of his chronicle, are not known. Events and dates going back to the Classical period and a century or so earlier are considered to be sound, or reasonably so. For the Dark Age and earlier, events and dates are increasingly questionable and increasingly mythological. Thus, the chronicle provides a Bronze Age date, as if for a real event, for a fight at Athens between the gods Poseidon and Ares.

3.1
The "Ages" that Hesiod refers to are philosophical notions set in poet-singer's language and are not necessarily the same as, and should not be confused with, the terms "Bronze Age" or "Iron Age" as used by archaeologists and historians.

4.1
In the Classical period certainly, and no doubt before, there were a number of works beside *Iliad* and *Odyssey* that dealt with the Trojan War. These stories are collectively referred to as the Homeric Cycle, or the Trojan Cycle, or the Epic Cycle. In addition to *Iliad* and *Odyssey*, these included Aethiopis, Sack of Ilium, Little Iliad, Returns, Telegony, and Cypria. For Cypria see Appendix D. Other than *Iliad* and *Odyssey*, these have not survived, and their contents are partially known only from summaries of a later age.

In the fog that shrouded the past for the Classical period Greeks, it was unclear to them which of these works Homer composed, and some thought that Homer composed all of them. Herodotus argued from certain facts that Homer could not have composed Cypria. Aristotle stated that Homer composed two works, *Iliad* and *Odyssey*, but elsewhere also attributed to him Margites, a comedy having nothing to do with the Trojan War. Aristotle attributed almost every compositional virtue to Homer's *Iliad* and *Odyssey*, but that does not prove that Homer composed either or both of these works. It only proves that *Iliad* and *Odyssey* were, in his view, meritorious. The fog referred to above still exists, because it is not certain even now if one man, Homer, composed both *Iliad* and *Odyssey*.

It has usually been assumed that *Iliad* and *Odyssey* were earliest, and that the others works mentioned above followed, but there is little or no justification for that view. No matter when any of these took final form in writing, it is likely that they all drew from the same undated body of lore that existed in the distant past before writing.

4.2
The best illustration of Greek fighting men of the Late Bronze Age is found on the so-called Warrior Vase from Mycenae. Two groups of men, apparently marching off to war, are shown. None of these men are clad in armor. Their primary protection is the shield. They appear to be wearing vests, which may be of linen layers, and that may have added some protection. From this vase, one does not get the impression that a Greek army of the Bronze Age marched off to war clad in bronze armor.

However, archaeology confirms that bronze armor did exist as is shown by a full suit of bronze armor found in a tomb at Dendra near Naplion, Greece. And certain Linear B tablets recording quantities of armor show a determinative, a sketch illustration of such armor.

It is likely that, as in most armies throughout much of history, there were two classes of fighting men in a Greek army of the Bronze Age. Those of higher status, and wealth, had the better armor and fought as heavy infantry or as mounted combatants. Others of lesser economic means fought as light infantry and without armor. Homer's *Iliad* deals with kings, princes, and others of high status to the near exclusion of lower classes. It is this upper class that would be expected to wear bronze armor. Thus, the frequent mention of bronze armor in *Iliad* is credible.

The illustration on the cover of this book is reasonably correct for the Bronze Age. A bronze-clad warrior is looking at the citadel of Troy in the distance. The citadel of Troy is illustrated accurately based on archaeological evidence. He carries a round shield. The Warrior Vase men carry round shields with bottom cut-outs, but other illustrations from the Bronze Age show the use of fully round shields which are thus authentic to the Bronze Age. On the shield an octopus is painted. These are illustrated in just this way on Bronze Age vases from Greece. He wears greaves (shin guards). So do the men on the Warrior Vase. He wears a bronze helmet. The men on the Warrior Vase wear some sort of helmet and that may be of bronze. On the whole, the illustration on the cover can be considered to be accurate for the Bronze Age.

5.1
The slight difference in spelling between Alaksandus and Alexandros would be due to the Hittite scribes, perhaps, who spelled the Greek name in their records poorly. It is also possible that the name Alaksandus is Anatolian, and that Greeks, hearing of the name Alaksandus of Troy, assimilated it to a name in Greek that made sense to them—Alexandros.

5.2
It is not surprising that linguistic experts would be unconvinced by the equation

Ahhiyawa=Acheoi or Ahhiyawa=Achaiwoi.

It is likely that in Mycenaean times, the Late Bronze Age, there was a name that was ancestor to the Homeric name Acheoi (Achaeans in English). The name would have been introduced by Greeks of the Bronze Age to the Anatolian west coast. There, it would have become familiar to those who spoke the Luvian language. Luvian-speakers would understand it and pronounce it with slight changes in accordance with their own speech patterns.

Hittites, an inland people, would have learned the name from those speaking Luvian. In turn, Hittites would introduce further pronunciation changes. The name was then committed to writing by the Hittites in a writing system which was far from perfect in representing the sounds of speech. As a result, the recording of the name by the Hittites would be significantly different from the original Greek pronunciation.

In Greece, Mycenaean culture died out, and with that the Mycenaean dialect of Greek also died away. Without writing, the Bronze Age name Achaiwoi was passed orally over the generations of the Dark Age, perhaps over five centuries, to Ionia and the time of Homer. Sound changes were bound to ensue. It is doubtful that a Greek of Homer's time would even have understood the speech of a Mycenaean Greek.

Thus the two names, though possibly originating from the same name of the Bronze Age, had diverged in place and time to such an extent that the equation above is beyond proof, even if valid.

5.3
In the Tawagalawas Letter, Hattusili tells the King of Ahhiyawa that he is prepared to offer Piyama-Radu a vassal position. "*Send Piyama back to me. I guarantee his safety. I will send the royal charioteer to pick him up.*" Those who do not accept that Ahhiyawa is primarily mainland Greece hold this to prove that Ahhiyawa cannot have been across the sea.

The solution can be seen in the following. Earlier, Piyama-Radu was in Millawanda/Miletus, an Ahhiyawa protectorate. The Hittite king had sought his extradition from Millawanda. The Ahhiyawa king directed Atpas, the Ahhiyawa governor of Millawanda, to make Piyama-Radu available to the Hittite king. When the king arrived in Milawanda to pick up Piyama-Radu, he discovered that Piyama-Radu had escaped by ship, possibly to an island under Ahhiyawa control. That escape certainly was facilitated by Atpas who was the son-in-law of Piyama-Radu.

The request for Piyama-Radu in the Tawagalawas Letter takes it for granted, without the need to say so, that the reverse process was to be used. Piyama-Radu was to be sent back to Milawanda. From there, the royal charioteer would take him to Hattusili.

6.1

The story is told in *Iliad*, of a time three generations before the Trojan War. Bellerophon was exiled from Greece, from the court of the king of Argos. He was given a folding tablet to be handed to his new host, the king of Lycia (Lukka) in the mountains in southwestern Turkey. On this tablet were secret instructions, written in "baneful symbols" that the bearer, Bellerophon, was to be killed once in Lycia. For this purpose, the king of Lycia sent Bellerophon on a supposedly suicidal mission. He was to slay the Chimera, a fire-breathing monster that dwelled in the nearby mountains. Rather than being killed, Bellerophon killed the monster.

Today, if one sails by night along the south shore of Lycia, there will be seen a fire burning night after night high on a mountain near the shore. From a beach below that mountain, one can take a trail on the mountain late in the day, and near the top of the trail toward night, a place is reached where flames are burning out of the mountainside. From a distance, these are seen as one flame. So it has been since before time. This is the Chimera, and the spot is so marked on a good map of Turkey.

The folding tablet referred to is a realistic item of the Late Bronze Age. Such a tablet was found by archaeologists in a Bronze Age ship wreck off the Lycian coast. The leaves of the tablet were originally coated with wax and writing was scribed onto the wax.

6.2
The matter of the dowry is suggested by Bryce in "Letter from a King of Ahhiyawa to a King of Hatti" appearing in Beckman and Bryce, see Readings. Whether or not it was a dowry, there was a gift of islands to the Greek king.

7.1
In early days of decipherment of Hittite documents, it appeared that the subject of the letter was Tawagalawas. Thus the name Tawagalawas Letter. Now it is recognized that Piyama-Radu is the subject with which the letter is concerned.

Tawagalawas was the brother of the Greek king. In a brief period of amity between the Greeks and the Hittites, as indicated by the letter, Tawagalawas had been a personal guest of the Hittite king.

7.2
As with many Hittite tablets, there is some damage leading to some unreadable text. That has allowed several interpretations, one of which is that the Hittites have gone to attack Wilusa. That interpretation makes little sense because there had always been good relations between the Hittites and Wilusa. Further, the Alaksandus Treaty bound the Hittites to come to the defense of Wilusa, and the Hittites took treaty obligations seriously.

7.3

Because the Tawagalawas tablet contains certain symbols hard to read because of damage, there has been some uncertainty that it is *Wilusa* that is written there. Hans Guterbock of the University of Chicago, a recognized authority on Hittite cuneiform texts writes, "The name of the town is slightly damaged, and the reading *Wi-lu-sa* has therefore been doubted. But an enlarged photograph ... shows the signs clearly enough, so that I do not hesitate to accept the reading. I thus take it as a fact that a Hittite king (most probably Hattusilis III in the middle of the thirteenth century) and a Great King of Ahhiyawa were at odds over the matter of Wilusa." See Readings, Guterbock, H. 1986.

7.4

It may be wondered, if the Piyama-Radu affair is the origin, or at least the primary origin, of the Trojan War story, why are not Piyama-Radu or Atpas mentioned in *Iliad*? Several reasons are likely.

As seems probable, Piyama-Radu and Atpas, having worked with Greeks for some time, probably also had Greek names in the blended Greek-Anatolian culture in which they lived. They may be in *Iliad* under a Greek name.

In any case, the tale of the battle at Troy was maintained for centuries by Greeks celebrating their own. This can perhaps be illustrated by recent events. Not long after World War II, movies and television documentaries began to appear in the United States celebrating the American assault on German-occupied Europe. Particularly featured were movies about the D-Day landings and the repulse of German forces. By such heroic means, American forces defeated Hitler. Of course, British and Canadian forces fought alongside. That is acknowledged. What of the USSR, the

Russians? Their role is recognized but it seems remote. The reason is, these war stories are about us, our forces, the valor of our predecessors. If it were not for history books, which constantly remind us of the Russian role in the war, knowledge of it might by now have faded from memory. In the days of Homer and before, there were no history books which told the whole story. Thus, memory of Piyama-Radu, or Atpas, or at least those names, might have rapidly faded away.

7.5

In *Odyssey*, there is mention of the Greek attack on Mysia, and here it is said that the Mysians were supported by their allies, the "Ketians in throngs." The resemblance of the term Ketian to the Egyptian Bronze Age term Kheta is noteworthy. This is the Egyptian term for the Hittites. Allowance must be made for differences in spelling systems and the effects of time. Thus, reference to Ketians in *Odyssey* may be a remnant memory of the Hittites in the Seha/Mysia, Wilusa/Troy battles. At least one translation of *Odyssey* into English simply refers to Hittites as a translation of Ketians. See Readings. Rieu, E. V.

7.6

Greek pottery was a kind of luxury ware, and has been found in archaeological remains in Greece, Anatolia, Crete, Cyprus, the Levant, Canaan, and Egypt. Shape and painted decoration had varied over the years of manufacture, changing from one style to another at certain times. Certain pottery styles can, in some cases, be correlated with Egyptian king-dates which are known with high accuracy. By this means, dates can be assigned to pottery styles and their changeover points. With this, the presence of certain styles of Greek pottery in an archaeological context can be used to establish absolute dates of that context. Under the right circumstances, this provides the gold standard for determining absolute dates in the Late Bronze Age for many lands along the eastern Mediterranean.

Depending on circumstances, problems with this approach are several and include: uncertainties in correlation of pottery styles with Egyptian dates; uncertainties that the changeover was synchronous in all places of Greek pottery manufacture; uncertainties that users stopped using an old style and took on the new style rather quickly; uncertainties in recognizing the style in a pottery fragment from a "dig" when only a few small fragments are found.

Why is pottery used for dating? There is nothing else. For the times and places discussed here, carbon dating is not used due to a lack of high quality organic specimens found in secure and certain archaeological contexts.

8.1
Although gods are mentioned in the Linear B tablets, there is little or no evidence of a family or a corporation of the gods as one later finds in *Iliad*, *Odyssey*, and *Theogony*. The idea that the gods formed a family or a corporation was ancient in Near East and may have come to the Greek world in the centuries when Greece was open to influences from the East. At the time that *Iliad* was composed, gods were understood to constitute a family. Though they were "Greek" gods, they did not belong exclusively to the Greeks. The gods went off on vacation and visited far off tribes, and attended their festivities. In *Iliad* Apollo supports Troy (and was earlier a Trojan god) and that is not strange. Yet here, *Iliad* is anachronistic. Even as Homer composed, or close to that time, Apollo was gaining acceptance among the Greeks as a god uniquely theirs, as shown by the early existence of a Greek shrine to Apollo on the island of Delos.

8.2

Most Bible scholars probably accept the so-called Documentary Hypothesis in one form or another. This hypothesis holds that tales in Genesis and Exodus, and possibly beyond, as we have them now, were formed by the merger of three and perhaps four earlier "documents." These documents in some cases may have been oral traditions rather than written texts. Many story doublets are evident. There are in the Bible different versions of the Creation, of Noah and the Flood, of the theophany on Mount Sinai. One touchstone that distinguishes certain sources is that one source refers to God (in Hebrew, El) and another to The Lord (in Hebrew, Yahweh). Only with careful reading or scholarly attention is the blending of separate sources evident.

9.1

Even in recent times in India, there have been non-literate individuals known as Bhopas who performed in religious dramas. Their performances are based purely on memory, not on creation during performance. One Bhopa describes his early training. He was only four years old when his father began his lessons. Every day, he had to learn ten to twenty lines by memory, and would be rewarded a sweet for his effort. One such religious work, the Dev Narayan, vastly longer that *Iliad*, was in recent years committed to writing. The task took a month of eight hour days. Presumably, the recorder had the great advantage of use of a typewriter. See Dalrymple in Readings.

9.2

Parry and Lord reported that the existence of writing destroyed the performance abilities of the poet-singer. The circumstances are not clear, because the Bosnia poet-singers, illiterate as they were, had been aware of writing for generations. In their stories of conflict, they mention written messages carrying orders. It is difficult to account for this matter, but it is likely as follows. The poet-singer, much more than the present day opera singer or theater performer, must have a high degree of self-confidence. It is this, and the appreciation shown by his audience, that enables him to draw forth, on the spot, the words and phrases of his performance from deep mental resources. The insistent presence of writing destroys his confidence because it is associated in his mind with elites, with people he thinks to be smarter than he, with a superior technology, such that can report of the past better than he can. His audience also drifts away, and he loses confidence and ability to work.

Parry and after him Lord believed that *Iliad* must have been committed to writing with Homer's participation. It is likely that, since they held that Homer could not have been literate, he must have dictated the text.

Appendix A

Hittite King Dates

Per O. Gurney, The Hittites. See Readings.

All dates are BC dates

Tudhaliya II	1390–1370
Arnuwanda I	1370–1355
Tudhaliya III	1355–1344
Suppiluliuma I	1344–1322
Arnuwanda II	1322–1321
Mursili II	1321–1295
Muwatalli II	1295–1271
Urhi-Teshub	1271–1264
Hattusili III	1264–1239
Tudhaliya IV	1239–1209
Arnuwanda III	1209–1205
Suppiluliuma II	1205–?

Appendix B

Certain historic persons of Late Bronze Age Anatolia mentioned in the text.

Alaksandus: king of Wilusa, a party to the "Alaksandus Treaty"

Atpas: son-in-law of Piyama-Radu, and governor of Milawata under the Ahhiyawa king

Attarissiyas: an aggressive military man operating with chariot forces in southwestern Anatolia

Manapa-Tarhunda: king of Seha River Land and vassal of the Hittites

Masturi: prince, then king, of Seha River Land after Manapa-Tarhunda

Piyama-Radu: a military adventurer and opportunist operating along the west coast of Anatolia

Tawagalawas: brother of Ahhiyawa king, known from Tawagalawas Letter

Uhha-Ziti: king in Arzawa

Appendix C

Linguistic Equations

These equations are neither proved nor disproved by linguistic theory

Left=Bronze Age Right=Classical

(1) Lukka=Lukioi (Lycians)

(2) Wilusa=Wilios=Ilios

(3) Milawata/Millawanda=Miletus

(4) Apasas=Ephesus

(5) Lazpas=Lesbos

(6) Ahhiyawa=Achaioi (Achaea[ns])

(7) Appaliuna=Apollon=Apollo

(8) Alaksandus=Alexandros (Alexander)

(9) Masturi=Mestor

(10) Attarissiyas=Atreus

(11) Tawagalawas=Etewoklewes=Eteocles

(12) Piyama-Muwas=Piramos/Priamos (Priam)

(13) Para-Ziti=Paris

(14) Taruisa=Troia

(15) Talawa=Tlos

(16) Pina=Pinara

Appendix D

Cypria and the Attack on Troy

Cypria is known only from a surviving summary of the post Classical period. It is considered to be part of the so-called Homeric Cycle or Trojan Cycle all of which works were once attributed to Homer. Later day ancient scholars appear to have discovered, or more likely invented, authors other than Homer for most of those works.[4.1]

It has usually been assumed that Cypria is a later work, later than *Iliad*, because it seems to carefully avoid duplicating or contradicting what is said in *Iliad* (though that avoidance is not perfect). That would seem to mean that the composer of Cypria had a knowledge of *Iliad*, which must therefore be earlier. That argument is not convincing, however. The story in Cypria covers much time and territory. It could not do this without leaving voids in coverage. If Cypria already existed in the time of Homer, he would aware of such voids. He might then have recognized that he could plan a great work that took place in a very limited place—Troy—and over a very limited time—a few weeks. Such could easily be squeezed into a void in the coverage of Cypria without interfering with Cypria. With that possibility, *Iliad* might be later that Cypria. That does not even require that Cypria was composed as a whole, or even in writing, in the time of Homer. Freely told tales relating to the Trojan War, which later entered written form, might have been commonplace in the time of Homer, and still Homer might have seen an opening among them for his own work.

The Story

Zeus has decided on war. He has not yet decided on the means to bring that about. Then an opportunity presents itself. The gods were attending a wedding feast. Through some oversight, the goddess Strife had been left off the invitation list. She is enraged and schemes to disrupt the affair. She has an apple of gold upon which is inscribed "to the fairest" and she rolls this amidst the goddesses Hera, Athena, Aphrodite. Each reach for the apple, sure it was meant for them.

Strife is now loose among the goddesses. Some decision must be made. Paris (Alexander), prince of Troy, is known to have an eye for feminine beauty. He is chosen to determine to whom the apple is intended. Aphrodite, thinking ahead, has secretly offered Helen, the most beautiful woman in the world, as wife to Paris. Unfortunately, she is already married to Menelaus, king of Sparta.

Paris outfits a ship and sails for Greece and in due course becomes the guest of Menelaus. Menelaus is called away on business to Crete. He directs that his wife, Helen, furnish Paris with all that he might need. In the absence of Menelaus, Aphrodite ensures a liaison between Paris and Helen. Helen decides to leave Menelaus and elope with Paris. They take all of Menelaus' treasures and set sail for Egypt (though that is not in Cypria), to Sidon, and finally for Troy.

Iris, messenger of Zeus, informs Menelaus of what has happened. He rushes home. With his brother, Agamemnon, an expedition against Troy is planned. The will of Zeus is being accomplished.

Agamemnon and Menelaus travel over Greece gathering men for the military expedition. Odysseus feigns madness in an attempt to dodge the call, but is found out. Warriors gather at Aulis, which is at a strait between Euboea and the Greek mainland. There, an omen is seen. A snake swallows eight baby birds and the mother. This is interpreted to mean that that the war would swallow up nine years.

The military expedition puts out to sea, bound for Troy, (under the guidance of Achilles according to other sources) and makes landfall on the Anatolian coast. A deadly battle takes place. Then it is discovered that a huge mistake has been made. The Greek force had landed not at Troy but Mysia (Teuthrania). After heavy losses, the Greeks withdraw.

The Greeks forces then disperse. Some time after, they gather again at Aulis for a second try to reach Troy. To get a good wind, there is an attempt to sacrifice Iphigeneia, daughter of Agamemnon, to the goddess Artemis. The fleet sails again and makes landfall by Troy and there is a battle. The Greeks send envoys to the Trojans demanding the return of Helen and the treasure. They are rebuffed. There are battles, and much raiding about the countryside, and Zeus schemes to remove Achilles from the battle.

There is much more, irrelevant detail, not reported here.

Appendix E

Archilochus on the other Troy

A text by this poet has been found on a papyrus fragment and has been restored by Dick Obbink. Archilocus tells of the mistaken attack on Mysia.

> *One doesn't have to call it weakness and cowardice, having to retreat, it it's under the compulsion of a god: no, we turned our backs to flee quickly: there exists a proper time for flight ... The fair-flowing river Kaikos and the plain of Mysia were stuffed with corpses as they fell. And being slain at the hands of the relentless man (Telephus), the well-greaved Achaeans turned off with headlong speed to the shore of the much-resounding sea. Gladly did the sons of the immortals and brothers, whom Agamemnon was leading to holy Ilium to wage war, embark on their swift ships. On this occasion, because they had lost their way, they had arrived at that shore. They set upon that lovely city of Teuthras* [Mysia], *and there, snorting fury along with their horses, came in distress of spirit. For they thought that they were attacking the high-gated city of Troy, but in fact they had their feet on wheat-bearing Mysia.*

Appendix F

Mestor

In a moment of bitterness, King Priam reflects on the war. He notes that three of his sons have been valiant champions of Troy. These were Hector, Alexander, Mestor. The rest of his fifty sons—Priam had several wives—were worthless.

As noted in Hittite records, Manapa-Tarhunda had a son named Masturi. It can be taken as certain that if the Greeks attacked Seha River Land where Masturi was a prince, he would have fought against the attackers. And he might have gone north with the Hittite army to Troy to aid in their defense.

The names, Mestor and Masturi are identical in consonants. The initial vowel follows the pattern of a/e in Ephesos=Apasas. As for the second vowel, this is simply a spelling problem for names whose pronunciations are no longer perfectly understood.

Unlike the many Greek names that have a recognizable meaning in Greek, such as Alexandros, names such as Nestor and Hector are somewhat mysterious in origin. Calvert Watkins, a specialist in Indo-European linguistics (see Readings) believes that Hector could be an Anatolian name. In that case, so might be the name Mestor. Thus Mestor=Masturi is perfectly reasonable, and Homer's Mestor may reflect the historic character Maturi.

Along the west coast of Anatolia in the Bronze Age, many Greeks lived. Some, arriving as adventurers, left their wives behind, if they had wives. They would have married Anatolian women. A hybrid culture would have resulted, and names of Anatolian origin could have given rise to some names as known from *Iliad*.

Appendix G

Refutations

There have been a number of arguments framed to show that Homer knew nothing of the Bronze Age. Some have been discussed, and this will add to the discussion.

Iron. Iron was first refined from its ores and fabricated into useful items in Anatolia during Hittite times. A king wrote to the king of the Hittites asking for an iron dagger, which in time he received—a coveted present. Iron is not often mentioned in *Iliad* and two instances have already been discussed. A third involves Pandaros. He is said to be a Lycian (Lukka), an Anatolian, and his name is Anatolian. It is he alone who shoots an arrow with an iron arrow head. That it is an Anatolian who has such arrows is fully consistent with the Late Bronze Age situation in which it was Anatolians (Hittites) who were masters of iron working.

Chariots. Very little is really known about the tactical use of the chariot in the Late Bronze Age. It should not be asserted that chariots were used in spear-brandishing charges, or only in that way. Most terrain was unfit for tactical employment of chariots. That would include rocky, rutted, marshy, and sandy situations. That happens to characterize much of the terrain around Hissarlik/Troy. If chariots had been brought along by the Greeks and the terrain found to be unsuitable, the smart commander would find some use of them. Ferrying combatants to the place of need at a moderate speed and dropping them off would enable reinforcement to be accomplished much faster that it could be done by foot. That is all *Iliad* describes.

Clatter. A warrior falls fatally wounded and his armor clatters about him. It is a frequent description in *Iliad*. It has been said that Homer had it wrong, that Greek warrior body protection was of some light corselet fabric, and that only. Such would not clatter when the warrior fell. Then, in a Bronze Age tomb at Dendra, Greece, a full set of segmented armor was found, like that of knights of the recent Middle Ages. Presumably, if the warrior of this tomb had such bronze armor, others did also. If a warrior wearing this armor fell in battle, there would certainly be a clatter.[4.2]

Funerals. Homer describes the funeral for Patroclus, a Greek. He is cremated. Critics say that Greeks of the Late Bronze Age did not cremate their dead, that that was a custom of a later time. Let it be accepted, however, that there was a war at Troy. What is to be done with the Greek dead? They could not be shipped home. They ought not to be buried by Troy. Superstitious Greeks knew that such soil was infested with hostile gods who favored Troy. Archaeological work at Hissarlik Hill shows that the Bronze Age residents there used cremation as did the Hittites. The solution seems obvious. Cremation, even in the Bronze Age, would be the sensible solution for the Greeks.

In all of the instances just reviewed, it seems that Homer had it right.

Appendix H

Doublets and Triplets

Iliad doublets

The city is sometimes Troy and sometimes Ilios. The terms are used interchangeably.

The river outside Troy is sometimes called Scamander and sometimes Xanthos.

The prince of Troy who started the whole thing is sometimes called Alexandros (Alexander) and other times Paris.

Hector's young son is named Astyanax but elsewhere the name is Scamander.

Iliad triplet

In *Iliad*, Homer refers to the Greeks indiscriminately as Achaeans, or Argives, or Danaans. These are not treated as separate groups. Rather, the terms are used to refer to the entire Greek host interchangeably. When so used, this is no good explanation for this multiplicity.

Attack triplet

Iliad tells of the attack on Troy. There is but one attack. There is also a near-withdrawal by order of Agamemnon.

In Cypria, there are two attacks. The first is on Mysia followed by a withdrawal. Agamemnon is the Greek leader. Later there is an attack on Troy.

In Greek legend there was, before the Trojan War, an attack on Troy by Heracles with 18 ships manned by fifty men each.

Appendix I

Evolution of the Troy story from the Bronze Age to the time of Homer.

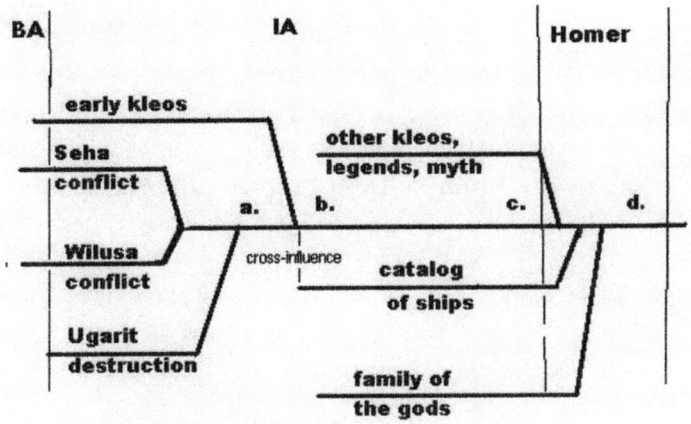

      a. War, destruction, at Wilusa/Troy
      b. Scope expansion, all Greece
      c. Ur-Ilias
      d. Homer's Iliad

From the Bronze Age to Homer, the story of Troy underwent changes as described in the text. Figure I shows one of many possible ways in which the original tale or tales became *Iliad*. The figure is based on a timeline, starting in the Bronze Age on the left, then the Iron Age, and terminating in the text of *Iliad* on the right.

On the left, there are the two core tales from which the tale of Troy began: the attack on Seha River Land/Mysia and the attack on

Wilusa/Troy. Since the actual conflicts happened closely spaced in time, they may have been joined as one story from the beginning.

The great city of Ugarit on the Syrian coast was sent up in flames toward the end of the Bronze Age. As the Greeks traded with cities of that coast, they would have quickly learned of the catastrophe. It would have impressed the poet-singers in Greece as a dramatic and useful tale. Probably few poet-singers would have known much geography and recognized the distinction and the distance between Ugarit and Troy. The story of this burning city may have been fused with the tale of the conflict at Troy. Or, if the poet-singers knew that Ugarit was distant from Troy, they may still have felt free to merge the tales as a matter of poetic license. The burning of Troy is not part of *Iliad*, but is mentioned in *Odyssey*. It is implicit in *Iliad* as the doom of the city is foreshadowed.

Early kleos refers to early stories of heroic deeds, perhaps performed by those at Seha River Land or Wilusa, but valorous deeds of other places or other times could have jointed the story of Troy at an early date.

The so-called Catalog of Ships represents a mystery. No matter when it was composed, it reflects knowledge of the evolving tale of Troy, since it needed to deal (mostly) in the same heroic names. Figure I suggests that the Catalog evolved as the story itself evolved. And as the story evolved, other kleos and myths joined the story.

The gods as a "family," as portrayed in *Iliad* and *Odyssey*, seems to be of a relatively late date, probably coming from the Near East in the Recovery period. It is best expressed in Hesiod's *Theogony*. Here, not only is the family described, but the "history" of the gods is described also. This description closely matches Near Eastern concepts.

Figure I is intended to represent only one concept of the growth of the story and merging of tales as appears in *Iliad*.

READINGS

Allen, T. W. 1969. *Homer: The Origins and the Transmission.* Oxford University Press.

Altschuler, E. L. et al. 2013. *Linguistic Evidence Supports Date for Homeric Epics.* Wiley Online Library.

Anderson, T. M. 1982. Atlakvida. *Dictionary of the Middle Ages*, Vol. 3. Scribners.

Anderson, T. M. 1982. Atlamal. *Dictionary of the Middle Ages*, Vol. 3. Scribners.

Anderson, T. M 1982. Nibelungenlied. *Dictionary of the Middle Ages*, Vol 3. Scribners.

Beckman, G. 1999. *Hittite Diplomatic Texts.* Society of Biblical Literature, Atlanta.

Beckman, G., T. and Bryce. 2011. *The Ahhiyawa Texts.* Society of Biblical Literature, Atlanta.

Andersson, Theodore M., and Stephen A. Barney. 1995. The Literary Character of Anglo-Saxon Poetry. In *Contradictions from Beowulf to Chaucer: Selected Studies of Larry D. Benson,* 1–14. Scolar, Aldershot, England.

Blegen, C., et al. 1953. *Troy 6th Settlement.* University of Princeton Press, Princeton, New Jersey.

Bloedow, E. 1988. The Trojan War and Late Helladic III C. *Praehistorische Zeitschrift* 63.

Boardman, J. 1964. *The Greeks Overseas.* Penguin, Harmondsworth, England.

Bryce, Trevor. 1989. Ahhiyawans and Mycenaeans-An Anatolian Viewpoint. *Oxford Journal of Archaeology* 8(3).

Burkert, W. 1995. Lydia Between East and West or How to Date the Trojan War: A Study in Herodotus. In *The Ages of Homer*, edited by J. B. Carter. University of Texas Press, Austin.

Caskey, J. L. 1948. Notes on Trojan Chronology. *AJA* 52(119–122).

Chadwick, H. M. 1912. *The Heroic Age.* Cambridge University Press, Cambridge.

Chadwick, J. 1958. *The Decipherment of Linear B.* Cambridge University Press.

Chadwick, N. K., and Zhirmuasky, V. 1969. *Oral Epics of Central Asia.* Cambridge University Press, Cambridge.

Collinder, B. 1964. *The Kalevala and its Background.* Almqvist and Wiksell, Stockholm.

Dalrymple, W. 2006. Homer in India. *The New Yorker* (November 20):48–55.

Dart, J. Henry, 1865. Iliad of Homer. Longmans, Green. London.

Davis, J. L. 1992. Review of Aegean Prehistory I: The Islands of the Aegean. *AJA* 96:699–756.

Desborough, V. R. d'A. 1964. *The Last Mycenaeans and Their Successors*. Clarendon Press, Oxford.

De Vet, T. 1996. The Joint Role of Orality and Literacy in the Composition, Transmission, and Performance of the Homeric Texts: A Comparative View. *Transaction of the American Philological Association* 126(43–76).

Dorsch, T, S., trans. 1965. *Aristotle: On the Art of Poetry*. Penquin, Middlesex.

Fagles, R. 1990, trans. *Homer. The Iliad*. Penguin Classics.

Finley, M. L. 1970. *Early Greece: The Bronze and Archaic Ages*. Norton, New York.

Finnegan, R. 1992. *Oral Poetry*. Indiana University Press, Bloomington.

Foley, John Miles. 1988. *Theory of Oral Composition*. Indiana University Press, Bloomington.

Ford, A. 1997. The Inland Ship: Problems in the Performance and Reception of Homeric Epic. In *Written Voices, Spoken Signs*, pp. 83–109. Harvard University Press, Cambridge, Massachusetts.

Fowler, R., ed. 2004. *The Cambridge Companion to Homer*. Cambridge University Press, Cambridge.

Friedrich, J. 1957. *Extinct Languages*. Dorset Press. New York.

Garstang, John, and Gurney, O. R. 1959. *The Geography of the Hittite Empire*. British Institute of Archaeology at Ankara, London.

Gurney, O. R. 1990. *The Hittites*. Penguin.

Guterbock, H. G. 1981. *The Hittites and the Aegean World: Part I, The Ahhiyawa Problem Reconsidered.* Archaeological Institute of America meeting record, East and West Great Moments of Contact.

Guterbock, H. G. 1984. Hittites and Achaeans: A New Look. *Proceedings of the American Philosophical Society* 128(2).

Guterbock, H. G. 1986. Troy in Hittite Texts? Wilusa, Ahhiyawa, and Hittite History. In *Troy and the Trojan War: A Symposium Held at Bryn Mawr College*, edited byMachteld Mellink. Bryn Mawr, Pennsylvania

Hanson, O. 1994. A Mycenaean Sword from Bogazkoy-Hattusa Found in 1991. *BSA* 89:213–215.

Haslam, M. 1997. Homeric Papers and Transmission of the Text. In *A New Companion to Homer*, edited by I. Morris and B. Powell. Brill.

Hawkins, J. D., and Easton, D. F. 1996. Hieroglyphic Seal from Troia. *Studia Troica* 6:111f.

Heinhold-Krahmer, Susanne. 1983. *Untersuchungen zu Piyamaradu. Orientalia* 52.

Herodotus. *History*.

Hiller, S. 1991. Two Trojan Wars? On the Destructions of Troy VIh and VIIa. *Studia Troica.* 1:145–154.

Hoffner, Harry H. 1980. Histories and Historians of the Ancient Near East: The Hittites. *Orientalia* 49:283–331.

Hopper, R. J. 1976. *The Early Greeks*. Harper and Row, New York.

Horrocks, G. 1997. Homer's Dialect. In *A New Companion to Homer*, edited by I. Morris and B. Powell. Brill.

Hurwit, J. M. 1989. Origins and Promises: Poet and Painter in the Dark Age. In *The Art and Culture of Early Greece, 1100–480 B.C.* Cornell University Press, Ithaca and London.

Huxley, G. L. 1960. *Achaeans and Hittites*. The Queen's University, Belfast.

Jablonka, P. 2000. Lower City. *Studia Troica* 10:28–30.

Janko, R. 1982. *Homer, Hesiod and the Hymns*. Cambridge University Press, Cambridge.

Janko, R. 1990. The Iliad and its Editors: Dictation and Redaction. *Classical Antiquity* 9(2):326-334.

Kirk, G. S. 1962. *The Songs of Homer*. Cambridge University Press, Cambridge.

Kolehmainen, J. I. 1973. *Epic of the North: The Story of Finland's Kalevala*. Northwestern Publishing Co., New York Mills, Minnesota.

Korfmann, M. 1992. Abstract. *Studia Troica* 2:124–125.

Korfmann, M. 1994. Datierung. *Studia Troica* 4:64–67.

Korfmann, M. 2005. Troya/Wilusa. Yayinlari.

Kullmann, W. 1984. Oral Poetry Theory and Neoanalysis in Homeric Research. In *Greek, Roman and Byzantine Studies* 25:307–323.

Langdon, M. K. 1975. The Dipylon Oinochoe Again. *American Journal of Archaeology* 79:139–140.

Lattimore, R. 1951. *The Iliad of Homer.* University of Chicago Press, Chicago.

Lord, A. B. 1964. *The Singer of Tales.* Harvard University Press, Cambridge, Massachusetts.

Lord, A. B. 1966. Gudo Mededovic, Guslar-Slavic Foklore: A Symposium. *Journal of American Folklore.*

Luckenbill, D. D. 1911. A Possible Occurrence of the Name Alexander in the Boghaz-Keui Tablets. *Classical Philology* (6)1:85f.

McCarter, P. K. 1975. A Phoenician Graffito From Pithekoussai. *American Journal of Archaeology* 79:140–141.

McCarter, P.K. 1975. *The Antiquity of the Greek Alphabet and the Early Phoenician Scripts.* Published by Scholars Press for Harvard Semitic Museum, Missoula, Montana.

Mee, C. 1978. Aegean Trade and Settlement in Anatolia in the Second Millennium B.C. *Anatolian Studies* 28:121–156.

Mellink, Machteld. 1983. Part 2: Archaeological Comments on Ahhiyawa-Achaians in Western Anatolia. *AJA* 87.

Montjoy, P. A. 1998. The Aegean-West Anatolian Interface in the Late Bronze Age. *Anatolian Studies* 48:33–36.

Murray, G. 1924. *Rise of the Greek Epic*. Oxford University Press.

Mylonas, G. E. 1964. Priam's Troy and the Date of its Fall. *Hesperia* 33:363–380.

Naveh, J. 1973. Some Semitic Epigraphical Considerations on the Antiquity of the Greek Alphabet. *American Journal of Archaeology* 77:1–8.

Nilsson, M. P. 1932. The Mycenaean Origin of Greek Mythology. Norton and Company. New York.

Notopoulos, J. A. 1960. Homer, Hesiod and the Achaean Heritage of Oral Poetry. *Hesperia* 29.

Nylander, C. 1963. The Fall of Troy. *Antiquity* 37:6–11.

Ottaway, J. H. 1991. New Assault on Troy. *Archaeology* 44(5) September/October.

Page, D. 1950. *History and the Homeric Iliad*. University of California, Berkeley.

Palaima, T. 2005. 'Archives' and 'Scribes' and Information Hierarchy in Mycenaean Greek Linear B Records. In *Ancient Archives and Archival Traditions*, edited by M. Brosius, pp. 153–194. Oxford University Press.

Palaima, T. G. 2006. *Wanaks* and Related Power Terms in Mycenaean and Later Greek. In *Ancient Greece: From the Mycenaean Palaces to the Age of Homer*, edited by S. Deger-Jalkotzy and I. Lemos.

Parry, Milman, 1971. *The Making of Homeric Verse*, edited by A. Parry. Clarendon Press, Oxford.

Powell, B. B. 1988. The Dipylon Oinochoe and the Spread of Literacy in Eighth-Century Athens. *Kadmos* 27:65–68.

Powell, B. B. 1991. *Homer and the Origin of the Greek Alphabet.* Cambridge University Press, Cambridge.

Rieu, E. V. 1984. Homer—The Odyssey. Penguin Books. Harmondsworth England.

Robbins, M. 2001. *Collapse of the Bronze Age: The Story of Greece, Troy, Israel, Egypt and the Peoples of the Sea.* Authors Choice Press.

Russo, J. 1997. Homer's Formula. In *A New Companion to Homer*, edited by I. Morris and B. Powell. Brill.

Sale, William M. 1993. Homer and Roland, Part I. *Oral Tradition* 8(1):87–142.

Sale, William M. 1993. Homer and Roland, Part II. *Oral Tradition* 8(2)381–384.

Seveinic, N. 1992. Troya. Turizm Yayinlari. Troya Yayıncılık Turizm.

Simson, R. H. 2003. The Dodecanese and the Ahhiyawa Question. *Annual of the British School at Athens* 98:203–237.

Singer, I. 1983. Western Anatolia in the Thirteenth Century B.C. According to the Hittite Sources. *Anatolian Studies* 33:205–217.

Smith, William Benjamin, and Miller, Walter. 1944. *The Iliad of Homer.* Macmillan. New York.

Snodgrass, A. 1998. *Homer and the Artists.* Cambridge University Press, Cambridge.

Sperling, J. 1991. The Last Phase of Troy VI and Mycenaean Expansion. *Studia Troica* 1:155f.

Steiner, G. 2007. The Case of Wilusa and Ahhiyawa. *Bibliotcha Orientalis* LXIV (September/December):589–612.

Subotić, D. 1932. *Yugoslav Popular Ballads.* Cambridge University Press, Cambridge.

Taylour, W. 1964. *The Mycenaeans.* Thames and Hudson, New York.

Ten Cate, H. J. H. 1971. Contact Between the Aegean Region and Anatolia in the Second Millennium B.C. In *Bronze Age Migrations in the Aegean,* edited by R. A. Crossland, pp. 141–161.

Thucydides. *The History of the Peloponnesian War.*

Tritsch, F. J. Bellerophon's Letter 1967. *ATTI Memorie Del Congresso Internationale Di Micenologie Roma,* October 1967.

Unal, A.1991. Two Peoples on Both Sides of the Aegean Sea: Did the Achaeans and Hittites Know Each Other? In *Essays on Ancient Anatolian and Syrian Studies in the 2nd Millennium B.C.,* edited by Prince Takahito Mikasa. Otto Harrassowitz, Wiesbaden.

Vermeule E. 1972. *Greece in the Bronze Age.* University of Chicago Press, Chicago.

Wace, A. J. B., and Stubbings, F. H., eds. *A Companion to Homer*. Macmillan, London.

Wadley, S. S. 1988. Singing for an Audience: Aesthetic Demands and the Creation of Oral Epics. *Resound* 7(2).

Wardle, K. et al. 2014. Dating the End of the Greek Bronze Age: A Robust Radiocarbon-Based Chronology from Assiros Toumba, *PLoS ONE* 9(9).

Watkins, Calvert. 1986. Language of the Trojans. *Troy and the Trojan War: A Symposium Held at Bryn Mawr College,* edited by Machteld Mellink. Bryn Mawr, Pennsylvania.

West, M. L. 1988. The Rise of the Greek Epic. *Journal of Hellenic Studies* cvii:151–172.

West, M. 1997. Homer's Meter. In *A New Companion to Homer*, edited by I. Morris and B. Powell. Brill.

West, M. L. 2003. Atreus and Attarissiyas. *Glotta* 77:262–266.

Willcock, M. 1997. Neoanalysis. In *A New Companion to Homer*, edited by I. Morris and B. Powell. Brill.

Woodward, R. D. 1997. *Greek Writing from Knossos to Homer*. Oxford University Press,

Woudhuizen, F. C. 2007. Reflexes of Western Anatolian Toponyms in the Linear B Texts. *Proceedings of the Dutch Archaeological and Historical Society,* Vols. 36–37.

INDEX

Achaean/Achaioi 61, 62, 135
Achilles 45, 46, 80, 81, 110, 139
Aegean 68, 70
Aeolic 11, 27, 86, 87
Agamemnon 6, 46, 47, 66, 80, 91, 96, 138
Agora of Athens 39
Ahhiyawa 54, 61, 63, 64, 66, 72, 121, 122, 123, 135
Ajax 45, 96
Alaksandus, king 59, 60, 121, 133, 135
Alaksandus Treaty 59, 60, 76
Alexander 46, 110,
alphabet 35, 36, 37
Amphidamas 97
Anatolia 1, 2, 11, 48, 50, 73
Apasas 54, 57, 135
Apollo, god 60, 61, 90, 100, 127
Appaliuna 60, 135
Archaeology at Hissarlik/Troy 81
Archilochus 38, 80, 109, 141
Aristarchus 112, 113
Aristotle 110, 119
Armor 120, 146
Arzawa 53, 56, 57, 64
Assuwa 69, 70
Assuwa Confederation 58, 64, 68, 69, 84
Athena, god 90
Athenian pottery 31
Athens 6, 10, 13, 39, 90, 101, 109

Atlakvida 92, 95
Atli, king 92, 93
Atpas 76, 123, 125, 133
Atreus 66, 135
Attarissiyas 65, 71, 85, 133, 135
Attila 93, 99
audience for performance 19, 22, 23
Aulis 80, 139
baneful symbols 32
Bellerophon 68, 91, 123
Blegen, C. 81, 82
boar's tusk helmet 89
body shield 89
Boeotia 27
Bogazkoy 50, 51
Bosnia 19, 128
Bronze 43, 44, 45, 120, 121
Bronze Age 2, 44, 87, 88, 121, 122
Bronze Age survivals 89, 90
Brunhilde 93
Byzantium text 113, 114
Calendar 30
Catalog of Ships viii, 150
chariot warfare 65, 88, 145
Chimera 123, 124
Chios 26, 27, 73, 107, 109
Classical Period 13, 28, 39, 48, 57, 108, 112
Classical Period names 57
Clazomenae 72

Colphon 72
composition in performance 18
Crete 33, 71
Cypria 42, 80, 81, 87, 91, 119, 137
Cyprus 33, 36, 56
Dark Age of Greece 9, 10, 28, 30, 42, 45, 86, 89. 90
date of destruction Troy 82, 83, 84
date of Homer 40, 41
date of writing in Greece 37, 40
decipherment of Hittite 51
decipherment of Linear B 7
Delos 100, 108, 127
Demodocus 19, 98, 105
dictating *Iliad* 104
Digamma 58
Dipylon Jug 38, 39
Documentary Hypothesis 128
Dorpfeld, W. 81, 82
doublets 91, 147
earthquake, fire at Troy 82, 83
effect of writing 25
Ephesus 57, 72, 135
Epic Cycle 119
Eteocles 67, 135
Etzel, king 93
Euboea 11, 87, 97
family of gods 150
Forrer. E. 61
funerals 146
Gla 6, 66
Great King 62, 63, 65, 66, 69, 125
Greek writing 35, 36, 37
Gunnarr, king 92
Gunther, king 93

Guterbock, H. 125
Hattusa 2, 51, 64, 69
Hattusili, king 75, 76, 78, 131
Helen 46, 75, 99, 138
Herodotus 28, 29, 75, 110, 119
Hesiod 28, 31, 43, 97, 98, 99, 119
Hexameter 16, 22, 118
Hipparchus 109
Hissarlik 48, 59, 81
Hittite, Hittites 1, 5, 29, 50, 52, 53, 57, 76, 77, 78, 84, 85, 117, 122, 124, 126, 145
Hittite archives/records/tablets 50, 51, 53, 59, 68, 75, 124, 125
Homer 17, 27, 45, 49, 104, 105
as poet-singer 16, 113
as transitional poet-singer 25, 26, 106
as writer 25, 26, 105, 106
Homeric Cycle 42, 108, 119, 137
Homeridae 107, 109, 112, 113
Hymn to Apollo 100, 105
Ibrahim Pasha 95
Iliad 31, 32, 34, 42, 101
Ilios 58, 59
India 128
Indo-European language 29, 51
Iolkos 6
Ion 88, 113
Ionia 58
Ionian/Ionic 13, 27
Iron 32, 145
Janko, R. 17, 103
Jebb, R. C. 48
Kaikos River 77, 141

Ketians 126
Kleos 150
Korfmann, M. 81
Kosovo, battle of 93, 94, 95
Lazpas 53, 57, 58, 77, 135
Lead sheets 37
Lesbos 11, 57, 58, 73, 77, 81, 86, 87, 135
LH IIIA2 71, 72, 83, 83
LH IIIB 46, 71, 72, 82, 83
LH IIIC 71, 83
Library of Alexandria 111, 112
Linear B 6, 7, 8, 50, 61, 73, 89, 120, 127
location of Troy 47, 48,
Lord, A. 17, 97, 103, 128, 129
Luckenbill, D. D. 60
Lukka 53, 56, 65, 68, 135
Luvian 1, 58, 122
Lycia, Lycians 56, 123, 124, 135, 145
Madduwatta 65, 85
Manapa-Tarhunda Letter 57, 58, 76, 77, 85, 133
Map A 4
Map B 12
Map C 55
Masturi 133, 135, 143
Mededovic, Avdo 20, 97, 98, 105
Meleager 91
Menelaus 46, 75, 80, 99, 138
merging of tales 95
Mestor 135, 143
Millawanda/Milawanda 54, 56, 135
Milawata 56, 65, 135

Miletus 57, 71, 73, 85, 135
Mursili, king 64, 65, 75, 131
Muwatall, kingi 59, 75, 76, 84, 131
My Brother, title 62, 63, 64
Mycenae 5, 6, 10, 44, 45, 46, 47
Mysia/Mycians 80, 126, 139, 141, 150
Nestor 5
Nestor's Cup 39, 40,
Nibelunglied 92, 93, 95
Nilsson, M. 89
Odysseus 45, 96
Odyssey 31, 32, 34, 81
orality 17, 19, 87
oral transmission 101
Orchemenus 66
Papyrus 37
Parian Marble 118
Paris (Alexander) 138
Parry, M. 17, 19, 20, 97, 103, 128, 129
Patroclus 88
paying the poet 98
Peisistratus 112
Peoples of the Sea 96
performance venue 99
Persians 13, 14, 109
Phoenicia/Phoenicians 13, 33
Phoenician alphabet 13, 35, 36
physical demands of performance 24, 101
Pindar 80, 107
Piyama-Radu 63, 75, 76, 77, 78, 86, 122, 123, 125, 126, 133
Plato 110, 111, 112

Poetic Eddas 92
poet-singers endurance 20, 24, 97, 98
poet-singers in Bosnia 19
pottery dating 34, 46, 70, 71, 82, 83, 126, 127
Priam 83
Ptolemies 110, 111
Pudu-Hepa, queen 78
Pylos 5, 6, 15, 66
Recovery Period 13
repeats 17, 18
Rhapsode 109, 110
Rhodes 72
Rig-Veda 102
Roland, Song of 94, 95
Schiemann. H. 48, 81
Seha River Land 53, 57, 76, 77, 80, 85
Semonides 109, 118
Simonides 27, 118
Socrates 109, 112, 113
source of wealth in palaces 7
Sparta 4, 138
Spartan king list 30, 47
Strife, goddess of 138
Taruisa 59
Tawagalawas Letter 63, 67, 77, 78, 122, 123, 124, 133, 135
Teuthrania 80

text fragments 110, 111, 113
Thebes 6
Theogony 103, 104, 127
Thessaly 27, 87
Thucydides 110
Tiryns 6, 10, 66
transmission of text 108
Traven, B. 115
Trojan Cycle 31, 113, 119, 137
Trojan War as fiction 87
Troy VI 82, 83
Troy VII 83, 84
Tubingin, university 81, 83
Tudhaliya, king 60, 69, 131
Ugarit 46, 150
Uhha-Ziti, king 64, 72, 133
Venetus A. 113
vulgate 111, 112, 113
Walmu, king 60, 85
Warrior Vase 120, 121
Wilios 58
Wilusa 53, 58, 59, 76, 78, 123, 125, 126, 135, 150
Wilusiya 58
Winged Words 15
Works and Days 31
writing 7, 25, 35
Zenodotus 112, 113
Zeus, god 90, 138
Zogic' D. 20

Printed in Great Britain
by Amazon

57130514R00099